THE CABALA

and

THE WOMAN OF ANDROS

BOOKS BY THORNTON WILDER

NOVELS
The Cabala
The Bridge of San Luis Rey
The Woman of Andros
Heaven's My Destination
The Ides of March
The Eighth Day

COLLECTIONS OF SHORT PLAYS
The Angel That Troubled the Waters
The Long Christmas Dinner

PLAYS
Our Town
The Merchant of Yonkers
The Skin of Our Teeth
Three Plays:
Our Town
The Skin of Our Teeth
The Matchmaker

Thornton Wilder

THE CABALA

and

THE WOMAN
OF ANDROS

Harper & Row, Publishers
New York, Evanston, and London

Library of Congress Catalog Card Number: 68–28228

K-S

THE CABALA

*To my friends at the American Academy
in Rome, 1920–1921
T.W.*

THE CABALA

BOOK ONE

FIRST ENCOUNTERS

The train that first carried me into Rome was late, overcrowded and cold. There had been several unexplained waits in an open field, and midnight found us still moving slowly across the Campagna toward the faintly-colored clouds that hung above Rome. At intervals we stopped at platforms where flaring lamps lit up for a moment some splendid weather-moulded head. Darkness surrounded these platforms, save for glimpses of a road and the dim outlines of a mountain ridge. It was Virgil's country and there was a wind that seemed to rise from the fields and descend upon us in a long Virgilian sigh, for the land that has inspired sentiment in the poet ultimately receives its sentiment from him.

The train was overcrowded, because some tourists had discovered on the previous day that the beggars of Naples smelt of carbolic acid. They concluded at once that the authorities had struck a case or two of Indian cholera and were disinfecting the underworld by a system of enforced baths. The air of Naples generates legend. In the sudden exodus tickets for Rome became all but improcurable, and First Class tourists rode Third, and interesting people rode First.

In the carriage it was cold. We sat in our overcoats meditating, our eyes glazed by resignation or the glare. In one compartment a party drawn from that race that travels most and derives least pleasure from it, talked tirelessly of bad hotels, the ladies sitting with their skirts whipped about their ankles to discourage the ascent of fleas. Opposite them sprawled three American Italians returning to their homes in some Apennine village after twenty years of trade in fruit and jewelry on upper Broadway. They had invested their savings in the diamonds on their fingers, and their eyes were not less bright with anticipation of a family reunion. One foresaw their parents staring at them, unable to understand the change whereby their sons had lost the charm the Italian soil bestows upon the humblest of its children, noting only that they have come back with bulbous features, employing barbarous idioms and bereft forever of the witty psychological intuition of their race. Ahead of them lay some sleepless bewildered nights above their mothers' soil floors and muttering poultry.

In another compartment an adventuress in silver sables leaned one cheek against the shuddering windowpane. Opposite her a glittering-eyed matron stared with challenging persistency, ready to intercept any glance the girl might cast upon her dozing husband. In the corridor two young army officers lolled and preened and angled for her glance, like those insects in certain beautiful pages of Fabre, who go through the ritual of flirtation under futile conditions, before a stone, merely because some associative motors have been touched.

There was a Jesuit with his pupils, filling the time with Latin conversation; a Japanese diplomat reverently brooding over a postage-stamp collection; a Russian sculptor sombrely reading the bony structure of our heads; some Oxford students carefully dressed for tramping, but riding over the richest tramping country in Italy; the usual old woman with a hen and the usual young American, staring. Such a company as Rome receives ten times a day, and remains Rome.

My companion sat reading a trodden copy of the London *Times*, real estate offers, military promotions and all. James Blair after six years of classical studies at Harvard had been sent to Sicily as archaeological adviser to a motion picture company bent on transferring the body of Greek mythology to the screen. The company had failed and been dispersed, and Blair thereafter had roamed the Mediterranean, finding stray employment and filling immense notebooks with his observations and theories. His mind brimmed with speculation: as to the chemical composition of Raphael's pigments; as to the lighting conditions under which the sculptors of antiquity wished their work to be viewed; as to the date of the most inaccessible mosaics in Santa Maria Maggiore. Of all these suggestions and many more he allowed me to make notes, even to the extent of copying some diagrams in colored inks. In the event of his being lost at sea with all his notebooks—a not improbable one, as he crosses the Atlantic on obscure and economical craft, not mentioned in your paper, even when they founder—it would be my confusing duty to make a gift of this material to the Librarian of Harvard University where its unintelligibility might confer upon it an incomputable value.

Presently discarding his paper, Blair decided to talk: You may have come to Rome to study, but before you settle down to the ancients you see whether there aren't some interesting moderns.

There's no Ph.D. in modern Romans. Our posterity does that. What moderns do you mean?

Have you ever heard of the *Cabala*?

Which one?

A kind of a group living around Rome.

No.

They're very rich and influential. Everyone's afraid of them. Everybody suspects them of plots to overturn things.

Political?

No, not exactly. Sometimes.

Social swells?

Yes, of course. But more than that, too. Fierce intellectual snobs, they are. Mme. Agaropoulos is no end afraid of them. She says that every now and then they descend from Tivoli and intrigue some bill through the Senate, or some appointment in the Church, or drive some poor lady out of Rome.

Tchk!

It's because they're bored. Mme. Agaropoulos says they're frightfully bored. They've had everything so long. The chief thing about them is that they hate what's recent. They spend their time insulting new titles and new fortunes and new ideas. In lots of ways they're medieval. Just in their appearance for one thing. And in their ideas. I fancy it's like this: you've heard of scientists off Australia coming upon regions where the animals and plants ceased to evolve ages ago? They find a pocket of archaic time in the middle of a world that has progressed beyond it. Well, it must be something like that with the Cabala. Here's a group of people losing sleep over a host of notions that the rest of the world has outgrown several centuries ago: one duchess' right to enter a door before another; the word order in a dogma of the Church; the divine right of kings, especially of Bourbons. They're still passionately in earnest about stuff that the rest of us regard as pretty antiquarian lore. What's more, these people that hug these notions aren't just hermits and ignored eccentrics, but members of a circle so powerful and exclusive that all these Romans refer to them with bated breath as the Cabala. They work with incredible subtlety, let me tell you, and have incredible resources in wealth and loyalty. I'm quoting Mme. Agaropoulos, who has a sort of hysterical fear of them, and thinks they're supernatural.

But she must know some of them personally.

Of course she does. So do I.

One isn't afraid of people one knows. Who's in it?

I'm taking you to meet one of them tomorrow, this Miss Grier. She's leader of the whole international set. I catalogued her library for her,—oh, I couldn't have got to know her any other way. I lived in her apartment in the Palazzo Barberini and used to get whiffs of the Cabala. Besides her there's a Cardinal. And the Princess d'Espoli who's mad. And Mme. Bernstein of the German banking family. Each one of them has some prodigious gift, and together they're miles above the next social stratum below them. They're so wonderful that they're lonely. I quote. They sit off there in Tivoli getting what comfort they can from one another's excellence.

Do they call themselves the Cabala. Are they organized?

Not as I see it. Probably it never occurred to them that they even constituted a group. I say, you study them up. You ferret it out, the whole secret. It's not my line.

In the pause that followed, fragments of conversation from the various corners of the compartment flowed in upon our minds so recently occupied with semi-divine personages. I haven't the slightest desire to quarrel, Hilda, muttered one of the Englishwomen. Naturally you made the arrangements for the trip as best you could. All I say is that that girl did *not* clean off the washstand every morning. There were rings and rings.

And from an American Italian: I says it's none of your goddam business, I says. Take your goddam shirt the hell outta here. He run, I tell you; he run so fast you don't see no dust for him he run so.

The Jesuit and his pupils had become politely interested in the postage stamps and the Japanese attaché was murmuring: Oh, most exclusively rare! The four-cent is pale violet and when held up to the light reveals a water-mark, a sea-horse. There are only seven in the world and three are in the collection of the Baron Rothschild.

Symphonically considered, one heard that there had been no sugar in it, that she had told Marietta three mornings running to put sugar in it, or bring sugar, although the Republic of Guatemala had immediately cut them, a few had leaked out to collectors, and that more musk-melons than one would have thought possible were sold annually at the corner of Broadway and 126th Street. Perhaps it was in revulsion against such small change that the impulse first rose in me to pursue these Olympians, who though they might be bored and mistaken, had at least, each of them, "one prodigious gift."

It was in this company then, and in the dejected airs of one in the morning that I first arrived in Rome, in that station that is uglier than most, more hung with advertisements of medicinal waters and more redolent of ammonia. During the journey I had been planning what I should do the moment I arrived: fill myself with coffee and wine, and in the proud middle of the night, run down the Via Cavour. Under the hints of dawn I should behold the tribune of Santa Maria Maggiore, hovering above me like the ark on Ararat, and the ghost of Palestrina in a soiled cassock letting himself out at a side door and rushing home to a large family in five voices; hurry on to the platform before the Lateran where Dante mixes with the Jubilee crowd; overhang the Forum and skirt the locked Palatine; follow the river to the inn where Montaigne groans over his ailments; and fall a-staring at the Pope's cliff-like dwelling, where work Rome's greatest artists, the one who is never unhappy and the one who is never anything else. I would know my way about, for my mind is built upon the map of the city that throughout the eight years of school and college had hung above my desk, a city so longed for that it seemed as though in the depth of my heart I had never truly believed I should see it.

When I arrived finally, the station was deserted; there was no coffee, no wine, no moon, no ghosts. Just a drive through shadowy streets to the sound of fountains, and the very special echo of travertine pavements.

During the first week Blair helped me find and fit out an apartment. It consisted of five rooms in an old palace across the river and within stone's-throw of the basilica of Santa Maria in Trastevere. The rooms were high and damp and bad Eighteenth Century. The ceiling of the salone was modestly coffered and there were bits of crumbling stucco in the hall, still tinted with faint blues and pinks and gilt; every morning's sweeping carried off a bit more of some cupid's curls or chips of scroll and garland. In the kitchen there was a fresco of Jacob wrestling with the angel, but the stove concealed it. We passed two days in choosing chairs and tables, in loading them upon carts and personally conducting them to our mean street; in haggling over great lengths of gray-blue brocade before a dozen shops, always with a view toward variety in stains and unravellings and creases; in selecting from among the brisk imitations of ancient candelabra those which most successfully simulated age and pure line.

The acquisition of Ottima was Blair's triumph. There was a

trattoria at the corner, a lazy casual talkative wine-shop, run by
three sisters. Blair studied them for a time, and finally proposed to
the intelligent middle-aged humorous one that she come and be my
cook "for a few weeks." Italians have a horror of making long-
term contracts and it was this last clause that won Ottima. We
offered to take on any man she recommended to help her with the
heavier work, but she clouded at that and replied that she could
very well do the heavier work too. The removal to my rooms must
have arrived as a providential solution to some problem in Ottima's life, for she attached herself passionately to her work, to
me, and to her companions in the kitchen, Kurt the police dog and
Messalina the cat. We each winked at the others' failings and we
created a home.

The day following our arrival, then, we called upon the latest
dictator of Rome and found a rather boyish spinster with an
interesting and ailing face, fretful bird-like motions and exhibiting
a perpetual alternation of kindness and irritability. It was nearly six
when we walked into her drawing-room in the Palazzo Barberini
and found four ladies and a gentleman seated a little stiffly about a
table conversing in French. Mme. Agaropoulos gave a cry of joy at
seeing Blair, the absent-minded scholar to whom she was so attached; Miss Grier echoed it. A thin Mrs. Roy waited until something had been dropped into the conversation about our family
connections before she could relax and smile. The Spanish Ambassador and his wife wondered how on earth America could get on
without a system of titles whereby one might unerrably recognize
one's own people, and the Marquesa shuddered slightly at the
intrusion of two coarse young redskins and began composing
mentally the faulty French sentence with which she would presently excuse herself. For a time the conversation blew fitfully

about, touched with the formal charm of all conversation conducted in a language that is native to no one in the group.

Suddenly my attention was caught by a tension in the room. I sensed the tentatives of an intrigue without being able to gather the remotest notion of the objectives. Miss Grier was pretending to babble, but was in reality quite earnest, and Mrs. Roy was taking notes, mentally. The episode resolved itself into a typical, though not very complicated, example of the Roman social bargain, with its characteristic set of ramifications into religious, political and domestic life. In the light of information received much later, I call your attention to what Mrs. Roy wanted Miss Grier to do for her; and what Miss Grier asked in return for her services:

Mrs. Roy had narrow eyes and a mouth that had just tasted quinine; while she spoke her ear-pendants rattled against her lean clavicles. She was a Roman Catholic, and in her political activity a Black of the Blacks. During her residence in Rome she had occupied herself with the task of bringing the needs of certain American charitable organizations to the attention of the Supreme Pontiff. Slander attributed a diversity of motives to her good works, the least damaging of which was the hope of being named a Countess of the Papal States. The fact is that Mrs. Roy was pressing audiences in the Vatican with the hope of inducing His Holiness to commit a miracle, namely to grant her a divorce under the Pauline Privilege. This consummation, not without precedent, depended upon a number of conditions. Before taking any such step the Vatican would ascertain very carefully how great the surprise would be in Roman Catholic circles; American cardinals would be asked in confidence for a report on the matron's character, and the faithful in Rome and Baltimore, without their being aware of it, would be consulted. This done it would be well to gauge the degree of cynicism or approval the measure would arouse in Protestants. Mrs. Roy's reputation happened to be above reproach, and her right to a divorce indisputable (her husband had offended under every category: he had been unfaithful; he had lapsed from a still greater faith; and he had become an *animae periculum,* that is, he had tried to draw her into an irreverent argument over the liquefaction of the blood of St. Januarius); but the Protestant *imprimatur* was needed. Whose opinion would be more valuable for this purpose than that of the austere directress of the American Colony? Miss Grier would be approached—and both women knew it—through channels exquisite in their delicacy and resonance; and if an uncertain note were sounded from the Palazzo Barberini, the familiar verdict Inexpedient would be returned to the petitioner, and the question never reopened.

Mrs. Roy having so much to ask from Miss Grier, wanted to know if there were any service she could render in return.

There was.

No Italian work of art of the classic periods may leave the country without an enormous export tax. How then did Mantegna's "Madonna between St. George and St. Helen" ever arrive at the Alumnae Hall of Vassar College without passing through the customs? It was last seen three years before in the collection of the poor Principessa Gaeta; it was so ascribed in the reports of the Minister of Fine Arts for the following years, in spite of the rumor that it was being offered to the museums of Brooklyn, Cleveland and Detroit. It changed hands six times, but the dealers, savants and curators were so taken up with the problem as to whether or not St. Helen's left foot had been retouched by Bellini (as Vasari affirms) that it had never occurred to them to ask if it had been registered at the border. It was finally bought by a mad old Boston dowager in a lavender wig who, dying, bequeathed it (along with three spurious Botticellis) to that college with which her vicious spelling alone would have prevented her association in any capacity save that of trustee.

The Minister of Fine Arts at Rome had just heard of the donation and was in despair. When the thing became known his position and reputation would be gone. All his vast labors for his country (*exempli gratia:* he had obstructed the disinterment of Herculaneum for twenty years; he had ruined the façades of twenty gorgeous Baroque churches in the hope of finding a Thirteenth-Century window; etc., etc.) would avail him nothing in the storms of Roman journalism. All loyal Italians suffer at the sight of their art treasures being carried off to America; they are only waiting for some pretext to rend an official and appease their injured honor. The Embassy was already in agonies of conciliation. Vassar could not be expected to give up the picture, nor to pay a smuggler's duty. Tomorrow morning the Roman editorials would picture a barbarous America stealing from Italy her very children and references would be made to Cato, Aeneas, Michelangelo, Cavour and St. Francis. The Senatus Romanus would sit on every bit of delicate business that America was endeavoring to recommend to Italian favor.

Now Miss Grier, too, was a trustee of Vassar. She had a flattering position in the long processions that formed in June among the sun-dials and educative shrubs. She was ready to pay the fine, but not until she had placated the city fathers. This could be done by obtaining the favorable votes of the committee that was to sit that very evening. This committee was composed of seven members, four of whose votes she already commanded; the other three were Blacks. For the matter to be dropped in the interest of the Princess Gaeta a unanimous verdict was necessary.

If Mrs. Roy descended at once to her car, she would have time to drive to the American College in the Piazza di Spagna and confer with dear omniscient Father O'Leary. Marvellous are the acoustics of the Church! Before ten that evening the three Black votes would be decently cast for conciliation. It was Miss Grier's task over the tea-table to convey this long exposition to Mrs. Roy and to intimate the ineffable return she, Miss Grier, would be able to make for any favors. This was complicated by the necessity of making sure that neither Mme. Agaropoulos nor the Ambassadress (men don't matter) suspected the least collusion. Fortunately the Ambassadress could not understand rapid French, and Mme. Agaropoulos, being sentimental, could be continually distracted from the main issue by little sops of prettification and pathos.

Miss Grier played these several cards with the economy and precision of a faultless technique. She had that quality which is a peculiar part of the genius that invests great monarchs, and which we see notably in Elizabeth and Frederick, the power of adjusting threats to just the degree that stimulates, yet does not antagonize. Mrs. Roy understood at once what was expected of her. She had been packing committees and conciliating soured Papal chamberlains and Italian political *dévotés* these many years; trading in influence was her daily portion. Moreover joy can exert the happiest sort of influence on the intelligence and she felt her divorce was at hand. She rose hastily.

Will you excuse me if I run? she murmured. I told Julia Howard I would call for her at Rosali's. And I have an errand in the Piazza di Spagna.

She bowed to us and fled. What emotion is it that lends wings to such matter-of-fact feet and blitheness to such thin dispositions? The next year she married a young French yachtsman, half her age; she settled down in Florence and gave birth to a son. The Blacks no longer talked votes when she entered their drawing-rooms.

Vassar retains the painting and in its archives a letter from the Italian Secretary for Foreign Affairs which reads like a deed of gift. The influence of a work of art upon the casual passerby is too suDtle for determination, but one has faith to believe that the hundreds of girls who pass beneath the Mantegna daily draw from it impulses that make them nobler wives and mothers. At least that is what the Ministry promised the College.

When the others had gone, Miss Grier made a face after them, lowered the lights and bade us talk about New York. She seemed to take some pleasure in such exotic company as ourselves, but her mind strayed until suddenly jumping up, she smoothed out the folds of her gown and bade us hurry off, dress, and come back to dinner at eight. We were surprised but equal to it, and dashed off into the rain.

At once I harried Blair for more facts about her. He could give me little; the portrait of her mind and even of her features lies in the following account of her ancestry that I made out for myself by reading between the lines and by studying the photographs of a history of the Griers, written by a second cousin, for considerations.

It seems that her great-grandfather had gone to New York in 1800, suffering from ill-health. He took an old house in the country and intended spending his days like a hermit, studying the prophetic passages of the Bible and encouraging the multiplication of four pigs that he had brought across the water in a basket. But his disposition improving with his affairs, he soon discovered himself to be married to the heiress of Dawes Corners, Miss Agatha Frehestocken, the death of whose parents, ten years later, united two farms of considerable extent. Their children, Benjamin and Anne, were brought up with such education as fell to them on rainy afternoons at the caprice of their father. Our Miss Grier's grandfather, a crafty single-minded country boy, disappeared for

many years into a whirlpool of obscure activity in town, becoming
in turn potboy, newspaper devil and restaurant manager. At last he
revisited his parents and forced them to permit his using their land
as security for some railroad investments. We have his picture at
this stage: the daguerreotype of the Dutch yokel with the protrud-
ing lower lip and grinning pugnacious eyes is reproduced in any
history of the great American fortunes. Probably the gentle art of
horsewhipping one's parents was revived that Sunday evening at
Dawes Corners for Anne intimates that she was directed to take
her knitting into the feed-house and sit on sacks until she was
recalled. The old father cursed the son roundly from the impre-
catory psalms and had his curious revenge: the worm of religious
introspection was stirred in the brain of Benjamin Grier and a
strain of ill-health in his body. Success came of it: he became a
deacon and a millionaire at about the same time; he was presently
directing five railroads from a wheel-chair. His parents died in a
Washington Square mansion, unforgiving to the end.

Benjamin married the daughter of another magnate, a girl who
in another age and faith would have retired to a convent and eased
the poverty of her mental and spiritual nature in a perpetual flow
of damp unexplainable tears. She bore a sickly son to the world of
brownstone, a son in whom the esthetic impulse, stifled during so
many generations of Griers and Halletts, attained a piteous flowering, a passion for the operas of Rossini, and for things he fondly
took to be Italian, garish rosaries, the costumes of the peasants of
Capri, and the painting of Domenichino. He married a firm sharp
woman, older than himself, who had deliberately chosen him in
the vestry of the Presbyterian Church. They were incredibly
wealthy, with that wealth that increases in the dark and, untended,
doubles in a year. With the affiliation of this determined Grace
Benham one last offspring was made possible to the Grier line,—

our Miss Grier. To the score of governesses that trod sobbing on one another's heels, she appeared a monster of guile and virulence. She was dragged without rest from New York to Baden-Baden, from Vevey to Rome, and back again; and she grew up without forming any attachment to place or person. Her parents died when she was twenty-four and finally sheer solitude did what exhortation could not do: her character softened in an attempt at piteously luring people to talk to her, live with her, to fill somehow the moneyed emptiness of her days.

Such an account of her extraction, if she read it, would have neither interested her nor embarrassed her. Her mind lay under the hot breath of a great fretfulness; she lived to ridicule and insult the fools and innocents of her social circle. In this fretfulness floated all the enthusiasms and frustrations of her line: her great-grandfather's gloom, her grandfather's whip and his dread of the Valley of Bones, her grandmother's red eyes and her father's repressed loves for the Normas and Semiramides of the Academy of Music. She was restless too, with the masculine capacities inherited from her grandfather, the capacities of a business magnate, that given her sex and situation could find their only outlet in a passion for making women tremble and a mania for interfering in the affairs of others. She was with all this a woman of intelligence and force; she ruled her eccentric and rebellious parish with acrid pleasure and at her death the drawing-rooms of Rome resounded with a strange wild murmur of muted joy.

Her portrait is not complete without an account of her strangest habit, due partly to the sleepless nights of a lifetime of illness, and partly to the fear of ghosts instilled in her by governesses when she was a girl. She was never able to sleep until the coming on of dawn. She feared to be alone; toward one in the morning she could be found urging her last callers to stay a little longer; *c'est l'heure*

du champagne, she would say, offering them that untimely in-
ducement. When finally they went away she would devote the rest
of the night to music, for like the German princes of the Eighteenth Century she maintained her own troup of musicians.

These sessions before dawn were not vaguely and sentimentally
musical; they were to the last degree eclectic. In one night she
would hear all the sonatas of Scriabin or the marches of Medtner;
in one night both volumes of the Well-Tempered Clavichord; all
the Handel fugues for organ; six Beethoven trios. Gradually she
won away from the more easily appreciated music altogether and
cultivated only what was difficult and cerebral. She turned to music
that was interesting historically and searched out the forgotten
rivals of Bach and the operas of Grétry. She paid a group of
singers from the Lateran choir to sing her endless Palestrina. She
became prodigiously learned. Harold Bauer would listen meekly to
her directions on phrasing Bach—he averred that she had the only
truly contrapuntal ear of the age—and the Flonzaleys acceded to
her request to take certain pages of Loeffler a little faster.

In time I encountered a number of people who for one reason or
another were unable to sleep between midnight and dawn, and
when I myself tossed sleepless or when I returned late to my rooms
through the deserted streets—at the hour when the parricide feels a
cat purring against his feet in the darkness—I pictured to myself
old Baldassare, in the Borgo, former Bishop of Shantung, Apos-
tolic Visitor to the Far East, rising at two to study with streaming
eyes the Church Fathers and the Councils, marvelling he said, at
the continuous blooming of the rose-tree of Doctrine; or of Stasia,
a Russian refugee who had lost the habit of sleeping after dark
during her experience as nurse in the War, Stasia playing solitaire
through the night and brooding over the jocose tortures to which
her family had been subjected by the soldiers of Taganrog; and of

Elizabeth Grier listening the length of her long shadowed room to some new work that d'Indy had sent her or bending over the score while her little troup revived the overture to *Les Indes Galantes*.

When we remounted the steps an hour later, then, we found the guests already arrived and awaiting their hostess. Among other privileges Miss Grier had long reserved to herself a prerogative of royalty, that of being the last arrival at one's own parties. In the hall the maître-d'hôtel gave me a note reading: Please take in Mlle. de Morfontaine, a high Merovingian maiden who may invite you to her villa at Tivoli. In a few moments Miss Grier had slipped in and was greeting her guests in a hurried zigzag across the room. She was dressed after a costume-plate by Fortuny, conceived in salamander red and black. About her neck hung a rare medal of the Renaissance, much larger than any other woman would have ventured to wear.

As this woman wanted to be in a position to hear every word spoken at her table Rome had long had good reason to complain of the crowded arrangements of her dinners; we were packed together like the hurried diners at Modane. But she had still other conventions to challenge: she discussed the food; she reversed the direction of conversation from the right to the left hand at the least convenient opportunities; she talked to the servants, chattily; she shifted the conversation from French to English or Italian capriciously; she referred to guests who had been invited but had not been able to come. One suddenly became aware that she was not eating the courses that were served to us. She began with a little bowl of breadcrumbs and walnuts; to this she added later— while we confronted a *faisan Souvaroff* dressed with truffles and *foie gras* and graced with that ultimate dark richness which it is the privilege of Madeira to confer on game—an American cereal,

soaked in hot water and touched with butter. Nor could she re-
strain herself from teasing her guests in a dangerous way, and with
almost inspired precision: a political Duke on his dull speeches;
Mrs. Osborne-Cady on the career as a concert-pianist that she had
sacrificed to a more than usually disappointing home-life. For a
moment at the beginning of the meal her electric eyes paused at my
place and she began to murmur ominously, but thinking better of
it she ordered the servant to offer me some more *oeufs cardinal*
adding with a sort of insolence that they were the only *oeufs
cardinal* that one could eat in Europe and that Mémé (the elder
Princess Galitzine) was a little fool to vaunt her chef, who had
received his training in railway-stations, etc., etc.

The high Merovingian maiden at my left was Mademoiselle
Marie-Astrée-Luce de Morfontaine, daughter of Claude-Elzéar de
Morfontaine and Christine Mézières-Bergh; her grandfather Comte
Louis Mézières-Bergh had married Rachel Krantz, the daughter of
the great financier Maxi Krantz, and had been the French ambassador to the Vatican in 1870. She was then, excessively rich, for
she owned, they said, more shares in the Suez Canal than the
Rothschilds: She was tall, large-limbed and bony, without somehow being too thin. Her high white face, framed between two
carnelian ear pendants, recalled some symbolical figure in a frieze
of Giotto, out of drawing, but radiating gaunt spiritual passions.
She had a hoarse voice and a rapt manner, and for the first ten
minutes said many foolish things because her mind was afar off;
one felt vaguely that it would come around in its own time. This it
presently did and with considerable impact. She outlined to me the
whole Royalist movement in France. She seemed to believe as
passionately in its aim as she depised its practice. There can be no
king in France, she cried, until catholicism has had a great revival

there. France cannot be great save through Rome. We are Latins; we are not Goths. They are forcing alien systems upon us. Eventually we shall find ourselves, our kings, our faith, our Latin hearts. I shall see France return to Rome before I die, she added clasping her hands before her chin. I replied faintly that both the French and Italian temperaments seemed to me singularly unrepublican, whereupon she laid her long pale hand upon my sleeve and invited me to come that week-end to her villa.

You will hear the whole argument, she said. And the Cardinal will be there.

I asked which Cardinal? The pain on her face showed me that at least for the circle in which she moved there were not seventy cardinals, but one.

Cardinal Vaini, of course. The College at present is singularly free of uninteresting priests, but surely the only cardinal with learning, with distinction, with charm, is Cardinal Vaini.

I had so often encountered learning, distinction and charm (to say nothing of piety) in the lower reaches of the Church that I was shocked to learn that these qualities were so rare higher up.

Besides she added, what other is friendly to France, the rebellious daughter? You have not yet met the Cardinal? Such knowledge! And to think that he will not write! If I may say it without disrespect His Eminence is afflicted with a sort of—inertia. The whole world is waiting for an explanation of certain contradictions in the Fathers; he is the only man who can do it; yet he remains silent. We beg him with prayers. It is in his power to effect the re-entry of the Church into literature. Perhaps he might single-handed carry through the cause we all have so at heart.

I asked shyly what cause this might be.

She turned toward me with some surprise. Why, the promulgation of the Divine Right of Kings as a dogma of the Church. We hope to have an Ecumenical Council called for that purpose within the next twenty-five years. I thought that of course you knew; in fact I assumed that you were one of our workers.

I replied that I was both an American and a Protestant, an answer that I felt relieved me of the burden of being a catholic royalist.

Oh, she said, we have many adherents who at first glance would appear to have no interest in the movement: we have Jews and agnostics, artists, and, yes, even anarchists.

I now felt quite sure that I was sitting beside an insane person. They don't lock you up when you have millions, I said to myself. The idea of trying to collect a Council, in the Twentieth Century, to give crowns a supernatural sanction and to enroll the sanction among the articles of obligatory belief, was no mere pious revery; it was lunacy. We were prevented from returning to the subject that evening, but several times I found her spacious half-mad glance resting on me with greater implication of intimacy than I was quite ready to acknowledge.

I will send the car for you at eleven, she murmured as she passed me in leaving the table. You must come. I shall have a great favor to ask of you.

On returning to the drawing-rooms I found myself beside Ada Benoni, daughter of a popular senator. Although she seemed almost too young to go out in the evening, she had that soft cautious sophistication of well-brought-up Italian girls. I asked her almost at once if she would tell me about the Cabala.

Oh, the Cabala's only some people's joke, she answered. There is no Cabala, really. But I know what you mean. And the young girl's eyes carefully estimated the distance between us and the

company on all sides. By Cabala they mean a group of people that
are always together and have a lot in common.

Are they all rich? I asked.

No . . . she answered thoughtfully. We mustn't speak so
loudly. Cardinal Vaini can't be rich, nor the Duchess d'Aquilanera.

But they're all intellectual?

The Princess d'Espoli isn't intellectual.

Then what have they in common?

Oh, they haven't anything in common, except . . . except that
they despise most people, you and me and my father and so on.
They've each got one thing, some great gift, and that binds them
together.

Do you believe that they work together and plan trouble here
and there?

The girl's forehead wrinkled and she reddened slightly. No, I
don't think they mean to, she said softly.

But they *do?* I insisted.

Well, they sit over there in Tivoli and talk about us and somehow, without knowing it, they then *do* something.

How many of them do you know?

Oh, I know all of them a little, she replied quickly. Everybody
knows all of them. Except, of course, the Cardinal. I love them all,
too. They're only bad when they're together, she explained.

Mlle. de Morfontaine has asked me to spend the week-end at
her villa in Tivoli. Will I see them there?

Oh, yes. We call that the hotbed.

Is it all right? Have you any advice to give me before I go?

No.

Yes, you have.

Well, she admitted, drawing her eyebrows together, I advise you to be . . . to be stupid. It's hard. You must expect them to be very cordial at first. They have a way of getting very excited about people and then getting tired of them and dropping them. Except every now and then they find someone they like and they adopt him or her for good, and there's a new member of the Cabala. Rome's full of people who went through the rapids and didn't stick. Miss Grier's especially that way. She's just met you lately, hasn't she?

Why, yes,—just this afternoon.

Well, she'll have you around every minute of the day for a while. She's coming over in a minute to ask you to stay to her midnight supper. She has famous midnight suppers.

But I can't. I was here to tea and immediately asked to dinner. It would be ridiculous to stay to midnight. . . .

It's not ridiculous in Rome. You're just getting into the rapids, that's all. Everybody cultivates their friendships in rushes. It's very exciting. Don't try and fight against it. If you do that you lose the best of everything. Do you want to know how I know about your being in the rapids? Well, I'll tell you. My fiancé was to have come to the dinner tonight, and an hour before, a note was brought to his house asking him to come next Friday instead and go to the Opera also. She does that often and it only means that she has found some new friend she insists on keeping by her that evening. Of course the second invitation, the consoling one, is always bigger and more showy than the first, but we get angry.

I should say so. I'm sorry I was the one to prevent . . .

Oh, that's all right, she answered. Vittorio's out waiting for me in the car now.

So it was that when Blair and I presented ourselves before Miss Grier to take our leave, she drew me aside with an irresistible vehemence and standing against my ear said: You are to come back here tonight. There will be some people in to a late supper whom I want you to meet. You can, can't you?

I made some show of protest, and the effect was appalling. But, my dear young man, she cried, I'll have to ask you to trust me. There is something of the first importance that I want to put to you. The fact is I have already telephoned a very dear friend of mine. . . . Please now, just as a favor to me, put off what you had planned. There's a very great service we want to ask you.

Of course with that I fairly folded up, as much with surprise as compliance. Apparently the whole Cabala wanted me to do favors.

Thank you, thank you so much. About twelve.

It was then about ten. Two hours to kill. We were about to go to the Circus, when Blair exclaimed:

Say, do you mind if I drop in and see a friend of mine for a minute. If I'm going Tuesday I ought to say goodbye and see how he is. Do you hate sick people?

No.

He's a nice fellow, but he hasn't long to live. He's published some verse in England; one of the thousand, you know. It got an awful rap. Maybe he's quite a poet, but he can't get over that diction. He's awfully adjectival.

We climbed down the Spanish Steps and turned in at the left. On the stairs Blair stopped and whispered: I forgot to tell you that he's watched over by a friend, a sort of water-colourist. They're dead-poor and it's all they can do to get a doctor. I meant to lend them some more money—what have you with you?

We assembled a hundred lire and knocked at the door. Receiving no answer we pushed it open. There was a lamp burning in the further of two mean rooms. It stood beside a bed and cast its light on the remorseless details of a barricade built during the last stages of consumption against a light vaulter; bowls and bottles and stained cloths. The sleeping invalid was sitting high in bed, his head turned away from us.

The artist must have gone out for a minute to look for some money, said Blair. Let's stay around a bit.

We went into the other room and sat in the dark looking at the moonlight that filled the Fountain of the Boat. There were fireworks on the Pincian Hill in memory of some battle on the Piave and the tender green of the sky seemed to tremble behind the Chinese blooms that climbed the night. A friendly tram entered the square at intervals, stopped inquiringly, and bustled out again. I tried to remember whether Virgil had died in Rome . . . no, buried near Naples. Tasso? Some piercing-sweet pages of Goethe, the particular triumph of Moissi who brings to them his wide-open eyes and elegiac voice. Presently we heard a call from the next room: Francis. Francis.

Blair went in: I guess he's gone out a minute. Can I do something for you? I'm going in a day or two and I called around to see how much better you are. Would it tire you if we sat with you a bit? . . . Come on in, say!

For the moment Blair had forgotten the poet's name and our introduction was slurred over. The sick man looked his extremity, but his fever gave to his eyes an eager and excited air; he seemed willing to listen or to talk for hours. My eye fell upon a rough pencilled note that lay on the table beyond the invalid's reach: Dear Dr. Clarke: he spat up about two cupfuls of blood at 2 P.M. He complained so of hunger that I had to give him more than you said. Be back at once. F.S.

Have you been able to write anything lately? Blair began.

No.

Do you read much?

Francis reads to me. He pointed to a Jeremy Taylor on his feet. You're Americans, aren't you? I have a brother in America. In New Jersey. I was to have gone over there.

The conversation lapsed, but he kept staring at us, smiling and bright-eyed, as though it were swift and rare.

By the way, are there any books you'd like us to lend you?

Thank you. That would be fine.

What, for instance?

Anything.

Think of one you'd like especially.

Oh, anything. I'm not particular. Only I suppose it would be hard to find any translations from the Greek?

Here I offered to bring in a Homer in the original and stammer out an improvised translation.

Oh, I should like that most of all, he cried. I know Chapman's well.

I replied, unthinking, that Chapman's was scarcely Homer at all, and suddenly beheld a look of pain, as of a mortal wound, appear upon his face. To regain control of himself he bit his finger and tried to smile. I hastened to add that in its way it was very beautiful, but I could not recall my cruelty; his heart seemed to have commenced bleeding within him.

Blair asked him if he had almost enough poems for a new book.

I don't think about books any more, he said. I just write to please myself.

But the insult to Chapman had been working in him; he now

turned his face away and great tears fell upon his hands. Excuse me. Excuse me, he said. I'm not well, and I seem to . . . to do this about nothing.

There was a search for a handkerchief, but none being found he was persuaded to use mine.

I don't want to go away without seeing Francis, said Blair. Do you know where I might find him?

Yes, yes. He's around the corner at the Café Greco. I begged him to go and get some coffee; he'd been here all day.

So Blair left me with the poet, who seemed to have forgiven me and was ready for the hazards of further conversation. Feeling it was better I did the talking, I began to discourse upon everything, on the fireworks, on the wildflowers of Lake Albano, on Pizzetti's sonata, on a theft in the Vatican library. His face showed clearly what matter pleased him; I experimented on it, and discovered that he was hungry for hearing things praised. He was beyond feeling indignant at abuses, beyond humor, beyond sentiment, beyond interest in any bits of antiquarian lore. Apparently for weeks together in the wretched atmosphere of the sick-room Francis had neglected to speak highly of anything and the poet wanted before he left the strange world to hear some portion of it praised. Oh, I laid it on. His eyes glowed and his hands trembled. Most of all he desired the praise of poetry. I launched upon a history of poetry, calling the singers by name, getting them wrong, assigning them to the wrong ages and languages, characterizing them with the worn epithets of an encyclopedist, and drawing upon what anecdotage I could,—all bad, but somehow marshalling the glorious throng. I spoke of Sappho; of how a line of Euripides drove mad the citizens of Abdera; of Terence pleading with audiences to come to him rather than to the tight-rope walkers; of Villon writing his mother's prayers before the great picture-book of a cathedral wall;

of Milton in his old age, holding a few olives in his hand to remind himself of his golden year in Italy.

Quite suddenly in the middle of the catalogue he burst out fiercely: I was meant to be among those names. I was.

The boast must have revolted me a little and my face have shown it, for he cried again: I was. I was. But now it's too late. I want every copy of my books destroyed. Let every word die, die. When I'm dead I don't want a soul to remember me.

I murmured something about his getting well.

I know more about it than the doctor, he replied, staring at me with stern fury. I studied to be a doctor. And I watched my mother and brother die, just as I am dying now.

There was no answer for that. We sat silent. Then in a gentler voice he said:

Will you promise me something? My things weren't good enough; they were just beginning to be better. When I am dead I want you to make sure that Francis does what he promised. There must be no name on my grave. Just write: Here lies one whose name was writ in water.

There was a noise in the next room. Blair had returned with the water-colourist. We withdrew. The poet was too sick to see us again and when I came back from the country he had died and his fame had begun to spread over the whole world.

BOOK TWO

MARCANTONIO

La Duchessa d'Aquilanera was a Colonna and came from the conservative wing of a family that cannot forget its cardinalitial, royal and papal traditions. Her husband had come of a Tuscan house that had received its illustration by the Thirteenth Century, was praised in the histories of Machiavelli and execrated in Dante. Neither family had counted a misalliance in twenty-two generations, and even in the twenty-third incurred only such stigma as attaches to marriage with an illegitimate Medici or a Pope's "niece." The Duchess could never forget—among a thousand similar honors—that her grandfather's grandfather, Timoleo Nerone Colonna, Prince of Velletri, had carried many an insulting message to the ancestors of the present King of Italy, the old but apologetic house of Savoy; and that her father had refused a Grandeeship at the court of Spain because it had been withheld from his father; and that through herself she carried to her son the titles of Chamberlain of the Court of Naples (if there were one), Prince of the Holy Roman Empire (if that superb organization had only survived) and Duke of Brabant, a title which unfortunately reappears among the pretensions of the royal families of Spain, Belgium and France. She had the best of claims to an Altesse, and even to an Altesse Royale; at least to the Sérénissime, for her mother had been the last member of the royal family of Craburg-Hottenlingen. She had the largest cousinage outside the Buddhist priesthood. The heralds of the European courts bowed to her with a particular distinction, realizing that by some accident many diverse and lofty lines converged in her odd person.

She was fifty when I met her, a short, black-faced woman with two aristocratic wens on the left slope of her nose, yellow, dirty hands, covered with paste emeralds (an allusion to her Portuguese claims; she was Archduchess of Brazil, if Brazil had only remained Portuguese), lame with the limp that pursues the Della Quercia, just as her aunt had been epileptic with the epilepsy of the true Vani. She lived in a tiny apartment in the Palazzo Aquilanera, Piazza Araceli, from the windows of which she watched the sumptuous weddings of her rivals, ceremonies to which she had been invited, but dared not attend, foreseeing that she would be assigned to places that fell below her pretensions; to accept a humble seat would be to admit that one had relinquished the whole bundle of vast historic claims. She had left many a great function abruptly on discovering that her chair was behind some of those Colonna cousins who had cast away all right to aristocratic distinction by marrying theatre women or Americans. She refused to be seated behind pillars among dubious Neapolitan titles—in the shadow of her own family tombs; to be left among the footmen at the door of a musicale; to be invited at the eleventh hour; and to be kept waiting in antechambers. For the most part she clung to her ugly stuffy rooms, brooding on the disregarded glories of her line and envying the splendors of her richer relatives. The fact is that from the point of view of a middle-class Italian she was not

really poor; but she was too poor to afford the limousine and livery
and great entertainments; to be without these and yet invested with
her pretensions was to be poorer than the last nameless body fished
out of the Tiber.

Recently however she had begun to receive unexpected and
thrilling recognitions. Little though she went out, when she did
appear in society, her austere face, her majestic limp, and her
strange jewels carried conviction. People were afraid of her. The
arbiters of precedence in Rome dared at last to intimate to the
Odescalchi and Colonna and Sermoneta that this almost shabby
little woman whom they snubbed and shoved like some half-wit
poor relation, had every right to precede them at a formal function. French circles, such as had not lost all seigneurial deferences
under the sponge of republicanism, recognized her ultramontane
alliances. She was the first to notice the improvement in her reception, and if a bit bewildered it did not take her long to set her sails
to the unexpected breeze. She had a son and daughter to advance
and it was for them that she now resolved to immolate her pride.
From the earliest signs of her rehabilitation she forced herself to
sally out into the world, and finding that her stock was higher in
the international colony she stooped distastefully to call upon the
American peeresses and on the South American representatives.
Eventually she found herself at Miss Grier's midnight suppers.
The reflection of the consideration she received in such places
finally reached her own people and she was gradually spared the
more obvious humiliations.

It became necessary for her now to drop her former friends, the
dull soured old women, more plaintive than herself, and with less
reason, with whom she had been accustomed to fret away the long
afternoons and evenings behind the drawn blinds of the Piazza
Araceli. She was obliged likewise to abandon a sordid habit that

linked her no less surely to the previous centuries, namely that of
rushing into law-suits. The innate capacity for affairs which
abounded in this woman had found during the days of her obscu-
rity this extraordinary outlet. She went about scenting out old
claims and deeds, the slips of tradesmen and the subtle omissions
of lawyers. She was always protecting her shyer friends from im-
position, and she was always successful and often made a good
deal of money. She employed obscure boy-lawyers and when she
was called upon as a witness, relying on her distinctions to prevent
her being interrupted, she used the occasion as an opportunity to
sum up the whole case. The middle classes seeing in the morning
paper that S. A. Leda Matilda Colonna duchessa d'Aquilanera was
attacking the City of Rome over the valuation of property near a
railroad, or contesting the bill of some popular stationer or
fruiterer on the Corso, suffered willingly the inconvenience of
holding a seat in court for hours in order to see the malignant
resourceful woman and to hear her trenchant sarcasms and her
irresistible accumulation of evidence. Yet her relatives had always
sneered at this passion, failing to see that she represented more
clearly than themselves the qualities that had always gone to char-
acterize the aristocracy.

It was this woman then whom we confronted when we returned
at midnight for our third engagement that day in the old palace.
Supper was served in a larger, brighter apartment than I had yet
seen. As I entered the huge doorway my eyes fell upon a strange
figure that I knew at once must be a Cabalist. A short, dark, ugly
woman, holding a cane between her knees was staring at me with
magnificent fierce eyes. With the bodiced dress and eagle's head I
became aware of her jewels, seven huge lumpy amethysts strung
about her neck on a golden rope. I was presented to this witch who

at once, and by the blackest art, made one like her. On hearing that Blair was leaving Rome shortly she centered her attention on me.

For a moment she sat before me, sliding the end of her stick nervously about on the floor, drawing in her upper lip, and gazing hard into my eyes. She asked me my age. I was twenty-five.

I am the Duchess d'Aquilanera, she began. What language shall we speak? I think we will talk English. I do not talk it good, but we must be plain. It must be so you must understand me quite perfectly. I am a great friend of Miss Grier. I have often talked over with her a great problem—a sorrow, my young friend—that is in my home. Suddenly tonight at seven o'clock she call me up on the telephone and told me she have found someone who could help me: she mean you. Now listen: I have a son of sixteen. He is important because he is somebody. How you say?—he is a personage. We are of a very old house. Our family has been in the front of Italy, everyone in her triumph and in her trouble. You are not sympathetic to that kind of greatness in America, not? But you must have read history, no? ancient times and the middle times and like that? You must realize how important the great families are . . . have always been to . . . countries . . .

(Here she grew nervous, and blew several bubbles and expended herself in those splendid Italian gestures denoting difficulty, perhaps futility, and resignation before the impossible. I hastened to assure her that I had great respect for the aristocratic principle.)

Perhaps you have and perhaps you haven't, she said at last. In all events, think of my son as a prince whose blood contains all sorts of kings and noble people. Well, now I must tell you he has fallen in bad ways. Some women have got hold of him and I do not know him any more. All our boys in Italy go that way when they are sixteen, but Marcantonio, my God, I do not know what is the matter with him and I shall go crazy. Now in America you are all descended from your Puritans, are you not, and your ideas are very different. There is only one thing to do, and that is: you must save my boy. You must talk to him. You must play tennis with him. I have talked to him; the priest has talked to him, and a good friend of mine, a Cardinal, has talked to him and still he does nothing but go to that dreadful place. Elizabeth Grier says that most boys in America at your age are just . . . naturally . . . good. You are *vieilles filles;* you are as temperate as I do not know what. It's very strange, if it's true, and I do not think I believe it; at all events it's not wise. At all events you must talk to Marcantonio and make him stay away from that dreadful place or we shall go mad. My plan is this: next Wednesday we are going for a week to our beautiful villa in the country. It is the most beautiful villa in Italy. You must come with us. Marcantonio will begin to admire you, you can play tennis and shoot and swim and then you can have long talks and you can save him. Now, won't you do that for me, because no one has ever come to you in such trouble as I have come to you in today?

Hereupon, in sudden fear that all her efforts had been in vain, she began waving her stick to attract Miss Grier's attention. That lady had been watching us from a corner of her eye and now came running up. The Duchess burst into a flood of tears, crying into her pocket handkerchief: Elisabetta, speak to him. Oh, my God, I have failed. He not want us and all is lost.

I was divided between anger and laughter and kept muttering into Miss Grier's ear: I'd be glad to meet him, Miss Grier, but I can't lecture the fellow. I'd feel like a fool. Besides what would I do with a whole week. . . .

She's put it to you wrongly, said Miss Grier. Let's not say anything more about it tonight.

At this the Black Queen began rolling about in her chair, the motions preparatory to rising. She rammed her stick against my shoe for leverage on the polished floor and stood up. We must pray to God to find another way. I am a fool. I do not blame the young man. He cannot realize the importance of our family.

Nonsense, Leda, said Miss Grier, firmly in Italian. Be quiet a moment. Then turning to me: Would you like to pass a week-end at the Villa Colonna-Stiavelli, or not? There's no stipulation about lecturing the Prince. If you like him, you'll feel like talking to him anyway, and if you don't like him, you're welcome to leave him alone.

Two Cabalists were begging me to take a glimpse of the most famous of Renaissance villas, one moreover that was obstinately closed to the public and that had to be peered at from the road half a mile away. I turned to the Duchess and bowing low accepted her invitation. Whereupon she kissed the shoulder of my coat, murmured with a beautiful smile: Christiano! Christiano! and bidding us goodnight, passed bowing from the room.

I shall see you Sunday at Tivoli, said Miss Grier, and tell you all about it there.

During the next few days my mind lay under the dread of the two engagements that lay ahead of me: the week-end at the Villa Horace and the missionary enterprise at the Villa Colonna. I stayed in my rooms, depressed, reading a little, or took long walks through the Trasteverine underworld, thinking about Connecticut.

The car that called for me Saturday morning already contained a fellow-guest. He introduced himself as M. Léry Bogard, adding that Mlle. de Morfontaine had offered to send for us separately, but that he had taken the liberty of requesting that we be called for together, not only because any company in crossing the Campagna is better than none, but because he had heard many things of me that led him to believe that we would not be uncongenial. I replied in that language wherein all courtesy sounds sincere, that the possibility of being congenial to so distinguished a member of the French Academy and to so profound a scholar was a greater honor than I dared hope for. These overtures did not tend to chill the encounter. M. Bogard was a fragile elderly gentleman, immaculately dressed. His face was delicately tinted by exquisite reading and expensive food, russet and violet about the eyes, his cheeks a pale plum from which rose the ivory-white of his nose and chin. His manner was soft and conciliatory, expressed for the most part in the play of his eyelids and hands, both of which fluttered in unison like petals about to fall upon the breeze. I spoke hesitantly of the pleasure I had derived from his works, especially from those pages, so faintly tinctured with venom, on Church History. But now he cried out at once: Do not mention them! My early indiscretions! Horrible! What would I not give to withdraw them. Can that nonsense have reached as far as America? You must let your friends know, young man, that those books no longer represent my attitude. Since then I have become an obedient son of the Church and nothing would give me greater comfort than to hear that they had been burned.

What may I tell my friends now represents your real views? I asked.

Why read me at all? he cried in mock grief. There are too many books in the world already. Let us read no more, my son. Let us seek out some congenial friends. Let us sit about a table (well-spread, pardi!) and talk of our church and our king and perhaps of Virgil.

My face must have shown a trace of the suffocation I experienced at this plan of life, for M. Bogard became at once more impersonal. The country we are traversing now, he said, has known stirring times . . . and he began an instructive travelogue, as though I were some stupid acquaintance, his hostess' son, and as though he were not, nor ever had been, a distinguished scholar.

On arriving at the Villa we were met by the steward and shown to our rooms. The Villa had been a monastery for many years and in purchasing it Mlle. de Morfontaine had obtained likewise the adjoining church which still served the peasants of the hillside. She claimed that the Villa was the very one that Maecenas had given to Horace: local tradition affirmed it; the foundations were of the best opus reticulatum; and the location fulfilled the rather vague requirements of classical allusion; even onomatopoeia testified, declared our hostess, asserting that from her window the waterfall could be literally heard to lisp

". . . domus Albuniae resonantis
Et praeceps Anio ac Tiburni locus et uda
Mobilibus pomaria rivis."

In furnishing her monastery our hostess had combined, as best she could, a delight in esthetic effects and a longing for severity. A long low rambling plaster building, without grace of line, was the Villa Horace. Disordered rose gardens surrounded it, with intentionally neglected gravel paths, and chipped marble benches. One entered a long hall at the end of which several steps descended to a library. The hall was lined with doors at regular intervals on both sides, doors to what had once been cells now thrown together into reception rooms. Many of these doors stood open during the day and the long corridor, paved with russet tile, was striped with the sunshine that fell across it. The ceiling had been coffered, and like the doors touched with dark green and gilt, and with that rich wasted brick-red that is the color of Neapolitan tiles. The walls were yellow white, of caked and crumbling plaster, and the beauty of the view with the optical illusion of distance and the depth and the lightness of the library seen like some great green-golden well at the further end, appealed to that sense of balance and one's tactile imagination as do the vistas in the paintings of Raphael whose spell is said to reside in that secret. To the left lay the reception rooms, carpeted in one color, hung with tabernacles and Italian primitives, while huge candelabra, pots of flowers and tables covered with brocades and crystals and uncut jewels, relieved the severity of unfreshened walls. Towards the end of the hall at the right one ascended a few steps to the refectory, the barest room in the house. By day the refectory was a meaningless casual club-room. Luncheon was a negligible affair at the Villa; one's conversation must be saved for dinner; at luncheon one barely looked at one another, one talked about the last rains and the next drought, or any subject that did not faintly allude to the devouring passions of the house, religion and aristocracy and literature. The beauty of the refectory was purely a matter of lighting and at eight o'clock the greatness of the room lay in the pool of wine-yellow light that was shed on the red table cloth, the dark green crested plates, the silver and the gold, the wineglasses, the gowns and decorations of the guests, the ambassadorial ribbons, the pontifical violets, and the little army of satin-clad footmen that suddenly appeared from nowhere.

On the night of my arrival the Cardinal was the last to appear at dinner, and entered directly into the refectory where we stood waiting for him. His expression was benignant, even beaming. While he blessed the meal, Mlle. de Morfontaine knelt on her admirable yellow gown and M. Bogard dropped on one knee and shaded his eyes. The grace was in English, a strange affair discovered by our erudite guest among the literary remains of some disappointed Cambridge parson.

> Oh, pelican of eternity,
> That piercest thy heart for our food,
> We are thy fledglings that cannot know thy woe.
> Bless this shadowy and visionary food of substance,
> Whose last eater shall be worm,
> And feed us rather with the vital food of
> Dreams and grace.

The Cardinal, though unimpaired in mind and body, looked all of his eighty years. The expression of dry serenity that never left his yellow face with its drooping moustache and pointed beard gave him the appearance of a Chinese sage that has lived a century. He was born of peasants on the plain between Milan and Como, and had begun his education at the hands of the local priests who soon discovered in him a veritable genius for latinity. He was passed upward from school to school gaining in his progress all the prizes the Jesuits had to offer. The attention of a large body of influential churchmen was gradually drawn to him and at the time of his graduation from the great college on the Piazza Santa Maria sopra Minerva (presenting a thesis of unparalleled brilliance and futility on the forty-two cases in which suicide is permissible and the twelve occasions on which a priest may take up arms without danger of homicide) a choice between three great careers was offered to him. The details of each had been prepared under the highest patronage: he might become a fashionable preacher; or one of the courtier-secretaries of the Vatican; or a learned teacher and disputant. To the amazement and grief of his professors he suddenly announced his intention of following a road that to them meant ruin; he declared for Missions. His foster-fathers raged and wept and called on heaven to witness his ingratitude; but the boy would hear of nothing less than the Church's most dangerous post in Western China. Thither in due time he departed with scarcely a blessing from his teachers who had already turned their attention to more docile if less brilliant pupils. Through fire, famine, riots, and even torture, the young priest labored for twenty-five years in the province of Sze-chuen. This missionary fever however did not entirely spring from piety. The boy, conscious of the great powers raging within him, had been throughout his youth insolent, contemptuous of his teachers and of his companions. He knew and despised every type of a churchman to be found in Italy; never had he seen a thing adequately done by them, and now he dreamed of a field of work where he would be answerable to no fool. In the whole realm of the Church there was only one region that filled his requirements; a month's travelling by crude wagon separates one from the next priest in Sze-chuen. There, then, after a shipwreck, some months of slavery, and other experiences that he never related, but which reached the world from his native helpers, he settled in an inn, dressed as a native, grew a pigtail, and lived among the villagers for six years without mentioning his faith. He passed the time studying the language, the classics, the manners, ingratiating himself with the officials and so perfectly identifying himself with the daily life of the city that in time he all but lost the odor of foreignness. When at last he began to declare his mission to those merchants and officials in whose homes he had become an almost nightly visitor his work was rapid. Perhaps the greatest of all the Church's missionaries since the Middle Age, he turned many a compromise that was destined to shock Rome profoundly. He somehow achieved a harmonization of Christianity and the religions and accepted ideas of China that had its parallel only in those daring readings that Paul discovered in his Palestinian cult. So subtle were the priest's adaptations that it never occurred to his first converts to be even conscious of repudiating their old faith until at last after twenty lectures he showed them how far they had gone and how charred were the bridges that lay behind them. Once he had them baptized however, he could give them only the bitterest bread to eat: the foundations of his cathedral lay squarely on a score of martyrs' graves, but once built suffered no further assault and grew slowly and irresistibly. Finally sheer statistics did what envy could not prevent and he was made a bishop. At the end of his fifteenth year in the East he returned to Rome for the first time and was received with cold dislike. His health had been partly undermined, and he was granted a year's repose, during which he worked in the Vatican library on a thesis relative to nothing in China, the donation of Constantine. This was considered shocking in a missionary and when it was published its learning and impersonality won it the neglect of the ecclesiastical reviewers. He was treated with condescension by the courtiers of the Palace; by implication they described to him their idea of his great creation in Western China: a low mud-brick meeting-house and a congregation of beggars who pretended to a conversion in order to be fed. He did not trouble to describe to them the stone cathedral with two awkward but lofty towers, the vast porch, the schools and library and hospital; the processions on Feast days carrying garish but ardent banners entering the great cavern of the Church and singing the correctest Gregorian; nor of the governmental honors, the tax-exemptions, the military respect during revolutions, the co-operation of the city.

At last he returned, willingly enough, to sink himself for another ten years into the remote interior. His visit to Rome had not altered his boyish attitude toward his fellowmen. He had heard strange tales about himself,—how he had amassed a huge fortune by taking bribes from the Chinese merchants, how he had interpreted the atonement in Buddhist terms and had allowed pagan symbols to be stamped upon the Host itself.

The ecclesiastical honors that eventually arrived must have been extravagantly deserved, for they came without his or any friend's negotiation. Sheer accomplishment must so have stared the Vatican in the face that it had felt torn from its hands the trophies it was accustomed to relinquish only on the receipt of petitions bearing ten thousand signatures or at the instance of wealth or power. To receive these new distinctions, the Bishop returned to Rome again after an absence of ten years. This time he meant to remain in Italy, having decided that henceforth his work would be better in the hands of natives. The ecclesiastics viewed this return with considerable trepidation, for if he returned as a scholar eager for doctrinal debates they dreaded seeing exposed their lack of interest or equipment; if he came as a critic of the Propaganda, they were all in danger. They watched him settle down with two Chinese servants and an absurd peasant woman whom he insisted on referring to as his sister, in a tiny villa on the Janiculum, join the Papal Archaeological Society and apply himself to reading and gardening. Within five years his retirement had become a greater embarrassment to the Church than his pamphlets might have been. His fame among Romanists outside Rome was unbounded; every distinguished visitor rushed from the station to get an introduction to the recluse of Janiculum; the Pope himself was a little tried by the zeal of visitors who imagined that His Holiness enjoyed nothing better than discussing the labors, the illness, and the modesty of the Cathedral Builder of China. English Catholics and American Catholics and Belgian Catholics who did not understand the exquisite subtlety of these matters and should let them alone, kept crying: Why isn't something being done for him? He humbly refused a high honorary Librarianship in the Vatican, but his refusal was not accepted and his name crowned the stationery; the same thing happened with the great committees on Propaganda; he did not appear at the meetings, but no speech was so influential as the report of chance words let fall in conversation with disciples at the Villino Wei Ho. His very lack of ambition frightened the Churchmen; they supposed it must arise from a similar emotion to that which kept Achilles sulking in his tent, and dreaded the moment when he would ultimately arise, swinging his mighty prestige and crush them for the honors they begrudged him; finally he was offered the Hat, by a committee from the College all in a perspiration lest he refuse it. This time he accepted their offer and went through the forms with a rigid decorum and with an observance of traditional minutiae that had to be elaborately explained to his Irish American colleagues.

It would be hard to say what his thoughts were those clear mornings as he sat among his flowers and rabbits, a volume of Montaigne fallen on to the gravel path from the tabouret beside him, what were his thoughts as he gazed at his yellow hands and listened to the hushed excitement of the Aqua Paola exclaiming in eternal praise of Rome. He must surely have asked himself often in what year his faith and joy had fled. Some said that he had become attached to a convert who had relapsed into paganism; some said that one day under torture he had renounced Christianity to save his life from the hands of brigands. Perhaps it was only that he had attempted the hardest task in the world and found it not so difficult after all; and reflecting that he could have built up a huge fortune in the financial world with half the energy and one-tenth the gifts; that he was the only person living who could write a Latin that would have entranced the Augustans; that he was the last man who would be able to hold in his head at one moment all the learning of the Church; and that to become a Prince of the Church required nothing but a devoted indifference to its workings,—reflecting on these things he may well have felt the world not to be worth the thunder of admiration and applause that was so continually mounting to Heaven in its praise. Perhaps one of the other stars is more worthy of one's best efforts.

Grace concluded, the meal could not be begun until the Cardinal was informed as to Alix. But where's Alix?

Alix is always late.

Are you sure she's coming?

She telephoned this afternoon, that . . .

Now isn't that too bad of her! She's coming in panting when the dinner's half over. Then apologies. Father, you're too kind to her. You always forgive her directly. You must act cross.

We must all act cross.

Everybody look angry when Alix comes in.

I had assumed that the conversation of the Cabala *in camera* would be vertiginous. If I anticipated the wit and eloquence of its table-talk I dreaded their gradual discovery that I was tongue-tied or doltish. When, therefore, the conversation at last broke forth I had the mixed sensation of discovering that it was not unlike that of a house party on the Hudson. Wait, I told myself, they will warm up. Or perhaps it is my presence here that prevents them from being at their best. I recalled the literary tradition that the gods of antiquity had not died but still drifted about the earth shorn of the greater part of their glory—Jupiter and Venus and Mercury straying through the streets of Vienna as itinerant musicians, or roaming the South of France as harvesters. Casual acquaintances would not be able to sense their supernaturalism; the gods would take good care to dim their genius but once the outsider had gone would lay aside their cumbersome humanity and relax in the reflections of their ancient godhead. I told myself that I was the obstacle, that these Olympians chattered and chaffed for a season until my departure, when the air would change,—what divine conversation. . . .

Presently in burst their Alix, the Princess d'Espoli, panting and a-flutter with apologies. She knelt to the Cardinal's sapphire. No one looked the least bit cross. The very servants beamed. We are to know a great deal about the Princess later; suffice it to say that she was a Frenchwoman of the utmost smallness and elegance, sandy-haired, pretty, and endowed with a genius for conversation in which every shade of wit, humor, pathos and even tragic power followed in close succession. Within a few moments she was enchanting the company with a lot of nonsense about a horse who had started talking on the Pincian Hill and the efforts of the Police Force to suppress such an aberration of nature. As I was presented to her she murmured quickly: Miss Grier told me to tell you that she will be here at about ten-thirty.

After dinner Mme. Bernstein played the piano for a time. She was still the power behind the great German banking house. Without ever venturing into her sons' offices or directors' meetings she yet disposed of all the larger decisions of the firm by curt remarks at their dinner tables, by postscripts to her letters and by throaty injunctions at the moment of saying goodnight. She wanted the sensation of having retired from its direction; her whole middle life had been expended in a magnificent display of generalship and financial imagination, yet she could not keep her mind off its problems. The friendship of the Cabala was beginning to reconcile her to advancing age, and drawing her further and further into her love for music.

As a girl she had often heard Liszt and Tausig in her mother's home; by dint of never playing Schumann or Brahms she had kept her fingers all silver and crystal, and even now, practically in her old age, she evoked the great era of virtuosi, a time when the orchestra had not led piano technique into a desperate imitation of brass and strings. Mlle. de Morfontaine sat holding in the cup of her hand the muzzle of one or other of her splendid dogs. Her eyes were filled with tears, but whether they were the facile tears of her half-mad nature or the witness of memories brought back on the tide of Chopin's sonata, we cannot know. The Cardinal had retired early and the Princess sat in the shadows, not listening to the music, but pursuing some of the phantoms of her most secretive mind.

Barely had the army with banners ceased drilling in the wintry sunlight of the last movement when a servant whispered to me that the Cardinal wished to see me.

I found him in the first of the two small rooms that had been set aside for him at the Villa. He was writing a letter, standing up to it at one of those high desks known to the clerks of Dickens and the illuminators of the Middle Age. I was later to receive many of those famous letters, never more nor less than four pages long, never falling short of their amazing suavity, never very witty nor vivid yet never untouched from beginning to end by the quality of their composer's mind. Whether he declined an invitation or suggested a reading of Freud's book on Leonardo, or gave suggestions on the feeding of rabbits, always from the first sentence he foresaw his last and always like a movement from Mozart's chamber-music the whole unit lay under one spirit and the perfection of details played handmaid to the perfection of the form. He seated me in a chair that suffered all the light that was in the room, treating himself to a fine shadow.

He began by saying that he had heard that I was to keep an eye on Donna Leda's son for a while.

I became warm and unintelligible in an effort at protesting that

I could guarantee nothing; that I was most reluctant; and that I still reserved the right to withdraw at any moment.

Let me tell you about him, he began. Perhaps I should say first that I am a sort of old uncle in the family, and their confessor for many years. Well,—this Marcantonio. What shall I say? Have you seen him?

No.

The boy is full of good things. He . . . he . . . Full of good things. Perhaps that's his trouble. You say you haven't met him yet?

No.

Everything seemed to start well. He was good in his studies. He made a lot of friends. He was particularly good in the ceremonial that his rank requires, his attendance at Court and at the Vatican. His mother was a little anxious about his boyish dissipations. She had his father in mind, I suspect, and wanted the boy to get over them as soon as possible. Donna Leda is a more than usually foolish woman. She was very pleased when he set up his own apartment off on the Via Po and became very secretive about it.

Here the Cardinal began to grope about again, perhaps surprised at his own awkwardness. Presently however he gathered up the reins with new determination and said: And then, my dear young man, something went wrong. We thought he would go through the usual experience of a Roman young man of his class and come out. But he has never come out. Perhaps you can tell me why this young fellow couldn't have had his five or six little affairs and gotten over it?

I showed myself as quite unequal to answering this question. In fact I was so amazed at the five or six little liaisons for a boy of sixteen, that it was all I could do to keep my face casual. I wanted badly not to appear shocked and endeavored by a lift of an eyebrow to imply that the boy might have a score if he liked.

Marcantonio, continued the priest, went around with a group of boys older than himself. His greatest wish was to be like them. You could see them at the races, in the music-halls, at Court, in the tea-rooms and hotel lobbies. They wore monocles and American hats, and all they talked about was women and their own successes. Euh . . . perhaps I should begin at the beginning.

There was a pause.

He was first initiated—perhaps I should use a stronger word— on Lake Como. He used to play tennis with some very warm little South American girls, heiresses from Brazil, I believe, from whom no secrets were hid. I fancy our Tonino merely meant to pay them a shy compliment or two, a sudden kiss under the laurel-bushes. But he soon found himself with a little . . . a sort of Rubens riot on his hands. Well, it began in imitation of his older friends. From imitation it went to an exercise of vanity. What was Vanity became Pleasure. Pleasure became a Habit. Habit became a Mania. And that's where he is now.

There was another pause.

You must have heard of how certain insane persons become enormously intelligent—that is, they become sly and secretive— trying to conceal their delusion from their guards? Yes; and I am told that vicious children perform feats of duplicity worthy of the most expert criminals, in an effort to conceal their tricks from their parents. You have heard of such things? Well, that is where Marcantonio is now. What can be done? Some people would say that we should let him go and make himself thoroughly sick. Perhaps they are right, but we should like to step in before that, if possible. Especially since there has come a new development into the story.

My mood at that moment was overwhelmingly against new developments. In the distance I could hear that Mme. Bernstein had resumed her Chopin. I would have given a lot for the power of being rude enough to leap for the doorknob and bid my host goodnight, a long goodnight to the wallowing little Prince and his mother.

Yes, continued the Cardinal, his mother has at last found a marriage for him. To be sure she does not believe there is a house in the world that can bring any new distinction to her own, but she has found a girl with an old name and some money and expects me to do the rest. But the girl's brothers know Marcantonio. They are in the group I described to you. They refuse to permit the marriage until Marcantonio has, well—been quiet for a while.

Now my face must have shown a rich mixture of horror and amusement and anger and astonishment, for the Cardinal became perplexed. You never can tell what will surprise an American, he probably said to himself.

No, no. Excuse me, Father. I can't, I can't.

What do you mean?

You want me to go to the country to hold him down to a few weeks of temperance. I don't understand how you can mean such a thing, but you do. He's a sort of Strassburg goose whom you want to stuff with virtue, don't you, against his marriage. Don't you see . . . ?

You exaggerate!

Excuse me if I sound rude, Father: No wonder you couldn't make an impression on the boy,—you didn't believe in what you were saying. You don't really believe in temperance.

Believe in it. Of course I do. Am I not a priest?

Then why not make the boy . . . ?

But after all, *we are in the world.*

I laughed. I shouted with a laughter that would have been insulting, if it hadn't contained a touch of hysteria. Oh, I thank thee, dear Father Vaini, I said to myself. I thank thee for that word.

How clear it makes all Italy, all Europe. *Never try to do anything against the bent of human nature.* I came from a colony guided by exactly the opposite principle.

Excuse me, Father, I said at last. I can't go on with it. Under any conditions I should feel an awful hypocrite talking to the boy. But if I knew it were only a measure to keep him good a month or two I should feel ten times more so. It can't be argued; it's just a matter one feels. I must tell Miss Grier I cannot visit her friend. She is driving out here at ten-thirty. If you will excuse me I shall go and find her in the music-room now.

Do not be angry with me, my son. Perhaps you are right. Probably I do not believe these things.

Hardly had I re-entered the music-room with my revolt written all over me when the Princess d'Espoli came forward. By that telepathy which the Cabala employed in its affairs she already knew that I had to be persuaded all over again. She made me sit down beside her and with the briefest outlay of those gifts of suppliance and enchantment of which she held the secret, she won my promise. In two minutes she had made it seem the most natural thing in the world that I should play stern older brother to a gifted drifting friend of hers.

As by the click of some invisible stage-manager Miss Grier entered.

How are you, how are you? she said, trailing her russet draperies across the tiles toward me. You can't guess who drove me out. I must hurry back. The Lateran choir is coming to sing Palestrina to me about twelve,—perhaps you know the motets from the Song of Songs? No? Marcantonio brought me here. He loves high-powered cars, and as his mother can't give him one I let him play with mine. Can you come out and meet him now? You'd better get your coat. Do you like night rides?

She led me out to the road where behind two blinding headlights a motor was humming impatiently. Antonino, she called.
This is an American friend of your mother's. Do show him the car
for half an hour, will you? Don't kill anybody.

An incredibly slight and definite little elegant, looking exactly
his sixteen years, with spark-like black eyes bowed stiffly to me in
the faint light over the wheel. Italian princes do not rise at the
approach of ladies.

Don't hurt my car or my friend, Marcantonio.

No.

Where are you going?

But he did not choose to answer and the aroused motor drowned
out the lady's questions. For ten minutes we sat in silence while the
road rose to the headlights. After a harrowing struggle with his
own selfishness Don Marcantonio asked me if I wanted to take the
wheel. Assured that nothing would alarm me more, he settled
down to driving with an almost voluptuous application. He made
nice distinctions with grades and corners, took long descents
cantabilemente, and played scherzi on cobblestones. The outlines of
the Alban hills stood out against the stars that like a swarm of
golden bees recalled that haughty Barberini who had declared that
the sky itself was the scutcheon of his house. All lights were out on
the farms, but occasionally we passed through a village whose
francobollo shop showed a lantern and a group of card players.
Many a wakeful soul in those enormous family beds must have
turned over, crossing himself, at the sighing whistle of our flight.

Presently however the driver wanted to talk. He asked a great
many questions about the United States. Could one plunge into the
life of the Wild West any minute? Were there many big cities as
big as Rome? What language was spoken in San Francisco? in
Philadelphia? Where did our athletes train for the Olympic
Games? Was the public allowed to watch them? Did I know about

such things? I replied that at school and college one couldn't help picking up hints on form and training. He then disclosed the fact that at the Villa Colonna he had directed the gardeners to make a running-track, cinders and hurdles and pit and shed and embanked corners. And that we were to use it every morning. He dreamed of himself doing incredible distances in incredible time. He outlined a plan to me whereby under my direction he would begin by running a mile every morning, and should add a half-mile daily for weeks. This would go on for years and then he would be ready to enter the Paris Olympics of 1924.

In my head the nerves of astonishment had been a little fatigued lately, what with Mlle. de Morfontaine and her Ecumenical Council, the Cardinal and his tolerances, Miss Grier and her cereals. But I confess they received no small twinge when this frail and emptied spirit announced his candidacy for a world's record in long runs. Not without sly intention I began to outline the sacrifices that such an ambition would entail. I touched on diet and early hours and early rising; he accepted them eagerly. I then skirted those self-denials that would touch him more particularly, and now with a mounting exaltation, with an almost religious fire, he pledged himself to all temperance. The fact that I was astonished shows my immaturity. I thought I was witness to a great conversion. I told myself that he wanted to be saved; that he was rolling up outside forces that might protect himself from his weakness; and that he hoped to find in athletics a deliverance from despair.

Returning to the Villa we found the company still listening to music. As we entered the room all eyes were turned towards us and I knew that for the present the Cabala had laid aside all activity and was brooding over one thing, the rescue of Donna Leda's son.

On arriving at my rooms in Rome I found several notes from a

Mr. Perkins of Detroit, a successful manufacturer who had crossed with me. Mr. Perkins, descending upon Italy for the first time, was resolved to see it at its best. There were no collections so private but that he was able to secure letters of admittance; no savants too occupied but that he obtained their services as ciceroni; audiences he obtained with the Pope were, as he called them, "super-special"; excavations not yet open to the public suffered his disappointed peerings. Some secretary at the Embassy must have mentioned that I had already made some Italian acquaintances, for there were these notes from him reminding me that he wanted to know some real Italians. He wanted to see what they were like in their homes, and he expected me to show him some. Mind, real Italians. I wrote him at once that all the Italians I knew were half French or half American, but assured him that when I had actually isolated a native I would bring them together. I added that I was leaving for the country, but would return in a week or two and see what could be done.

To the country then I went, being driven for the greater part of a day by Marcantonio himself. His enthusiasm for running had by no means abated; in fact it seemed to have gone from strength to strength, probably because of some lapses from strict training in the interval. It was late afternoon and a red sunset was filtering through a blue dusk when we entered the great gates of the park. There was first a forest of oaks; then a mile of open lawn with some hurrying sheep; then a pineta with a brook; the farmhouses in a cloud of doves; the upper terrace with a perspective of fountains; and at last the casino with the Black Queen trailing her garments of dusty serge across the driveway of powdered shell. There was little time to admire the orange-brown front of the villa roughened with wreaths and garlands that were crumbling away before the sun and rain, or the famous frieze of the women in Ariosto's poems, recalling the days when Pope Sylvester Lefthand held here his academy and invented the Sylvestrian sonnet-form. All I could do was to conceal my pleasure at the discovery that I was to live by candle-light in rooms that though the originals of hundreds of bad copies on Long Island, were here the secret shame of their owners. My hosts' ideal of residence was a hotel on the Embankment and they all but breathed an apology for the enormous rooms to which I was conducted, and in which I stood transfixed, lost in antiquarian dreams until Marcantonio knocked on the door to call me to supper.

At table I was presented to Donna Julia, Marcantonio's half-sister, and to a spinster cousin of the family, always present, always silent and whose lips never ceased moving, as solitaries' must, to the measure of her inner thoughts. Like all girls of her class Donna Julia had never been alone for more than a half-hour in all her life. Her immense talents for being bad had been balked at every turn; they had been forced to take refuge in her eyes. She had never even been allowed to read anything more inflammatory than the comedies of Goldoni and I Promessi Sposi, but she guessed at a criminal world and presently when marriage suddenly opened up to her every freedom she played her part in it. Donna Julia was a little stiff, almost ugly with her level baleful regard. She kept silent most of the time, was utterly incurious of me, and seemed chiefly occupied in angling for her brother's evasive glance so as to plant into it a triumphant significant idea.

One retired early at the Villa Colonna. But Marcantonio, for whom my simplest remarks were astonishing, would stop in at my room and talk for hours over some glasses of Marsala. No doubt his mother, noting the visits through her half-opened door down the hall, assumed with great satisfaction that I was reading lectures on hygiene. But, especially as the week advanced, we were chiefly taken up with a diagram that showed day by day how the little champion had run and in what time.

It must have been at the end of a week of this that in one of our late conversations his friendliness suddenly turned into contempt. A week's preoccupation with unsentimental matters now took its revenge. Back into his mind flooded the images of passion, and he wanted to boast. Perhaps he saw that prowess on the field was not to be his, and his egoism being athirst for all possible superlatives, he must replace it with a catalogue of the first prizes he had won in another arena. He recalled the Brazilian girls under the arbors of Como. He described how he had returned to Rome after that initiation bent on seeing whether the game was as easy as it had seemed. Suddenly his eyes had been opened to a world he had not dreamed of. So it was true that men and women were never really engaged in what they appeared to be doing, but lived in a world of secret invitations, signals and escapes! Now he understood the raised eyebrows of waitresses and the brush of the usher's hand as she unlocks the loge. It is not an accident that the wind draws the great lady's scarf across your face as you emerge from the door of the hotel. Your mother's friends happen to be passing in the corridor outside the drawing-room, but not by chance. Now he discovered that all women were devils, but foolish ones, and that he had entered into the true and only satisfactory activity in living— the pursuit of them. One minute he was exclaiming at the easiness of it; the next he described its difficulties and subtlety. Now he sang the uniformity of their weakness and now the endless variety of their temperaments. Next he boasted of his utter indifference and his superiority to them; he knew their tears but he did not believe they really suffered. He doubted whether they had souls.

To incidents that were true he added others that he wished had been true. To his acquaintance with a corner of Rome he added a fourteen-year-old's vision of a civilization where no one thought about anything but caresses. This fantasy took him about two hours. I listened without a word. It must have been this that undermined his exhilaration. He had been talking to impress me. Impressed I certainly was; no New Englander could help it; but I knew that a great deal depended on my not showing it. Perhaps it was his sudden realization that, seen through my eyes, these adventures were not enviable; perhaps it was that the black tide of reaction licked close on the heels of such pride; perhaps it was just truth finding room for utterance in his mounting fatigue,—at all events, there was strength left for one more outburst: I hate them all! I hate it. There's no end to it all. What shall I do? And he fell on his knees beside the bed and buried his face in the side of the mattress, his hands feverishly pulling at the cover.

Priests and doctors must often hear the cry Save me! Save me! I was destined to hear it from two other souls before my Roman year was over. Who now thinks it uncommon?

I scarcely know what I said when my turn at last came around. All I know is that my mind whipped up to its subject with a glee. Heaven only knows what New England divines lent me their remorseless counsels. I became possessed with the wine of the Puritans and alternating the vocabulary of the Pentateuch with that of psychiatry I showed him where his mind was already slipping: I pointed out wherein he already resembled his uncle Marcantonio, no mean warning; I made him see that even his interest in athletics was a symptom of his distintegration; how that he was incapable of fixing his mind on the general interests of man, and how everything he thought and did—humor, sports, ambition—presented themselves to him as symbols of lust.

My little tirade was effective beyond all expectation and for a

number of reasons. In the first place, it had the energy and sincerity which the Puritan can always draw upon to censure those activities he cannot permit himself,—not a Latin demonstration of
gesture and tears, but a cold hate that staggers the Mediterranean
soul. Again, all my words had already their dim counterpart in the
boy's soul. It is the libertine and not the preacher who conceives
most truly of the ideal purity and soundness, because he pays it
out, coin by coin, regretfully, knowingly, unpreventably. All my
words went to rejoin their prototypes in Marcantonio's mind.
Again, how could I know that he had arrived but recently at that
stage of failure when one's whole being reverberates, as with some
bell of despair, with the words: I shall never get out of this. I am
lost. Again, I found out later that Marcantonio had a streak of
religious frenzy in him, that for a year he had watched himself
alternating communion and dissipation, the exaltation of the former itself betraying him into the latter and the despair of the latter
driving him in anguish to the former. At last in sheer cynicism,
after watching himself fail so often, he had missed Mass for
several months. All these reasons go toward explaining the pros-
trating effect my brief and vindictive speech had. He cowered
against the carpet, begging me to stop, gasping out his promises of
reform. But having brought him to a conviction he might never
attain again, I thought it unwise to let go. I had reserves of
indignation left. But now he knelt crying on the carpet, covering
his ears with his hands and shaking his wet face at me with all its
terror and suppliance. I stopped and we stared at one another,
darkly, trembling under our several headaches. Then he went to
bed.

The next morning he seemed etherialized, made almost trans-
parent by his new resolutions. He walked lightly and with an air
of humility. No reference was made to the scene of the evening

before, but his glances over the tennis net implied an obedience and a deference that were more annoying than impudence. After two sets we wandered over to the lower fountain and here stretched out on the semi-circular bench he slept for three hours. It seemed to me as I watched morning advance to noon and the sun penetrate his thin body in the delicious fatigues that follow hysterical outbursts, it seemed that it would not be rash to wonder if possibly we may have succeeded. I day-dreamed. From the formal terrace below the casino came the click of topiary shears; from the field where the ancient altar had been placed, drum-shaped and bearing an almost effaced frieze, came the shouts of some divinity students (to whom a little villa on the estate had been offered as a vacation house) playing football, their cassocks tucked up about their knees; from the pine wood the exclamations of two shepherds who sat whittling while their flock drifted almost imperceptibly to the road beyond. The fountain before me gave forth its varied sounds: the whir of its initial jet and the tinkle as it fell back into the first bowl; the drumtaps as this overflowed and slipped into the second; and the loud loquacity with which the lowest basin received all that came to it from every level. Tacitus lay unread upon my knee while my eyes followed the lizards that flashed in and out of the brilliant sunshine on the gravel, noting their confusion when a sudden breeze bent the poised veil of the fountain and swept us all with a fine mist. The monotony of light and the noise of water, of insects, and of doves in the farmhouses behind me, combined to recall those tremulous webs of sound that modern composers set shimmering above their orchestra, to draw across it presently on the oboes their bleating melody in thirds.

While I sat there a note was brought me from the house. Mr. Perkins of Detroit had heard I was at the Villa and from the hotel in the nearby town announced his intention of calling on me,—

lucky in having a pretext for entering the most inaccessible villa in Italy. I scribbled on the back of his envelope that an unfortunate event in the family prevented my asking him to the house at present.

The hot sunlight of the morning had gathered its storm and all afternoon we sat indoors. Marcantonio and Donna Julia attempted teaching me the Neapolitan dialect, while the silent cousin sat by, deeply shocked. But my lesson soon descended into a subtle and barbed quarrel between the teachers. It was conducted for the most part in rapid and hate-laden parentheses, far above my head, in their thick *argot*. What she taunted him about I can only guess. He was invariably beaten; he grew loud and angry. Twice he leaped around the table to strike her; she waited for the blow, stretching herself sleekly and looking up at him from her magnetic eyes. At length he urged me to come away from her and to go upstairs, and the two parted much as children of seven would with a bout of grimaces and a competition to have the last ugly word.

After dinner the war was resumed. The Duchess was nodding by the fire; the cousin was mumbling opposite her. And the two children sat in the shadows exchanging invective. I was made strangely uneasy by their curious quarreling. I excused myself and went to bed. The last thing I saw was an infuriated blow that Marcantonio directed at his sister's shoulder and the last sound I heard was the tremolo of her provocative laughter as they tussled on the carved wooden chest in the corner. I debated with myself on the stairs: surely I had imagined it; my poor sick head was so full of the erotic narratives of the week; surely I imagined the character of mixed love and hate in those blows that were savage caresses, and that laughter that was half sneer and half invitation.

But I had not imagined it.

At about three I was awakened by Marcantonio. He was still

dressed. He poured at my drowsy head a torrent of whirling words in which I distinguished nothing but a feverish reiteration of the phrase: You were right. Then he left the room as abruptly as he had come.

What luck Mr. Perkins had always had! Even now when he brought to bear all his American determination and broke into the gardens of the forbidden Villa, what guardian angel arranged that he should see the Villa at its most characteristic? Surely a rich old Italian villa is at its most characteristic when a dead prince lies among the rosebushes. When Frederick Perkins of Detroit leapt the wall in the crystal airs of seven in the morning, he discovered at his feet the body of Marcantonio d'Aquilanera, 14th prince and 14th duke of Aquilanera and Stoli, 12th duke of Stoli-Roccellina, marquis of Bugnaccio, of Tei, etc., baron of Spenestra, of Gran-Spenestra, seigneur of the Sciestrian Lakes; patron of the bailly of the order of San Stephano; likewise prince of Altdorf-Hotten-lingen-Craburg, intendant elector of Altdorf-H-C.; prince of the Holy Roman Empire, etc., etc.; chamberlain of the court of Naples; lieutenant and cousin of the Papal Familia; order of the Crane (f. class); three hours cold, and with a damp revolver clutched in his right hand.

BOOK THREE

ALIX

The Cabalists received the news of Marcantonio's death philosophically. The account of it which the bereaved mother gave to Miss Grier was a miracle of misunderstanding. According to her I had done wonders; in fact it was the suddenness and thoroughness of the boy's reformation that had broken his health. She, *she,* was to blame. She should have foreseen that continence was not to be expected of a mere lad; he had gone insane from an excess of virtue and shot himself from too much sanctity. These things are out of our hands, dear Leda, murmured Miss Grier. The Cardinal made no comment.

The Cabala went back to its usual occupations. Being the biographer of the individuals and not the historian of the group I shall not take up much space here with details of the discomfiture of Mrs. Pole (she had been impudent to Miss Grier), nor of the Renan performance (*L'Abbesse de Jouarre* was effectively not given as a benefit at the Constanzi). From a purely disinterested love of Church tradition they blocked the canonization of several tiresome nonentities that had been proposed to gratify the faithful

in Sicily and Mexico. They saved the taxpayers of Rome the pur-
chase of hundreds of modern Italian paintings, and the establish-
ment of a permanent museum for them. They interested public
opinion in the faint smell of drains that is wafted through the
Sistine Chapel. When an oak forest fell ill in the Borghese
Gardens no one but the Cabala had the sense to send to Berlin for
a doctor. To tell the truth their achievements were not very considerable. I soon saw that I had arrived on the scene in the middle
of the decline of their power. At first they thought they could do
something about the strikes, and about the Fascismo, and the
blasphemies in the Senate; and it was only after a great deal of
money had been spent and hundreds of persons ineffectually
goaded that they realized that the century had let loose influences
they could not stem, and contented themselves with less preten-
tious assignments.

I came to see more and more of them. My youth and foreignness
never ceased to amuse them and they were made almost uncomfortable by the knowledge that I so liked them. They thought they
had outgrown being susceptible to being liked. From time to time
they would point their fingers to where I sat staring at them in
sheer wonder.

He's like an eager dog with his tongue out of his mouth, Alix
d'Espoli would cry. What does he see in us?

He never loses hope that we will suddenly say something
memorable, said the Cardinal looking at me musingly,—the look
of a great talker who knows that for lack of a Boswell his greatness must die with him.

He comes from the rich new country that will grow more and
more splendid while our countries decline to ruins and rubbish
heaps, said Donna Leda. That's why his eyes shine so.

Why, no, cried Alix. I believe he loves us. Just simply loves us

in a disinterested new world way. Once I had a most beautiful
setter, named Samuele. Samuele spent all his life sitting around on
the pavement watching us with a look of most intense excitement.

Did he bite? asked Donna Leda who had a literal mind.

You didn't have to give Samuele a sandwich to win his devotion. He liked to like. You won't be angry with me if every now
and then I call you Samuele to remind me of him?

You mustn't talk about him in front of him, muttered Mme.
Bernstein who was playing solitaire. Young man, get me my furs
from the piano until these people remember themselves.

The Princess explained me. What fairer service can one render
another? How could I do other than attach myself to one with so
quick and gracious an interpretation.

The Princess was not really modern. As scientists gazing at
certain almost extinct birds off Australia are able to evoke a whole
lost era, so in the person of this marvellous princess we felt ourselves permitted to glimpse into the Seventeenth Century and to
reconstruct for ourselves what the aristocratic system must have
been like in its flower.

The Princess d'Espoli was exceedingly pretty in a fragile Pari-
sian way; her vivacious head, surmounted by a mass of sandy
reddish hair, was forever tilted above one or other of her thin
pointed shoulders; her whole character lay in her sad laughing eyes
and small red mouth. Her father came of the Provençal nobility
and she had spent her girlhood partly in provincial convent schools
and partly climbing like a goat the mountains that surrounded her
father's castle. At eighteen she and her sister had been called in
from the cliffs, dressed up stiffly and hawked like merchandise
through the drawing-rooms of their more influential relatives in
Paris, Florence, and Rome. Her sister had fallen to an automobile
manufacturer and was making the good and bad weather of Lyons;

Alix had married the morose Prince d'Espoli who had immediately
sunk into a profounder misanthropy. He remained at home sunk in
the last dissipations. His wife's friends never saw or referred to
him; occasionally we became aware of him, we thought, in her late
arrivals, hurried departures and harassed air. She had lost two
children in infancy. She had no life, save in other people's homes.
Yet the sum of her sufferings had been the production of the
sweetest strain of gaiety that we shall ever see, a pure well of
heartbroken frivolity. Wonderful though she was in all the scenes
of social life, she certainly was at her finest at table, where she had
graces and glances that the most gifted actresses would fall short
of conceiving for their Millamonts, and Rosalinds and Célimènes;
nowhere has been seen such charm, such manners, and such wit.
She would prattle about her pets, describe a leave-taking seen by
chance in a railway station, or denounce the Roman fire depart-
ments with a perfection of rendering of Yvette Guilbert, a purer
perfection in that it did not suggest the theatre. She possessed the
subtlest mimicry, and could sustain an endless monologue, but the
charm of her gift resided in the fact that it required the collabora-
tion of the whole company; it required the exclamations, contradictions, and even the concerted shouts as of a Shakespearean mob,
before the Princess could display her finest art. She employed an
unusually pure speech, a gift that went deeper than a mere aptitude
for acquiring grammatical correctness in the four principal languages of Europe; its source lay in the type of her mind. Her
thought proceeded complicatedly, but not without order, in long
looping parentheses, a fine network of relative clauses, invariably
terminating in some graceful turn by way of climax, some sudden
generalization or summary surprise. I once accused her of speaking
in paragraphs and she confessed that the nuns to whom she had
gone to school in Provence had required of her every day an oral

essay built on a formula derived principally from Madame de Sévigné and terminating in a *concetto*.

Such rare personalities are not able to derive nourishment from ordinary food. Rumors of the Princess's strange stormy loves reached us continually. It seems that she was doomed to search throughout the corridors of Rome a succession of attachments as brief and fantastic as they were passionate and unsatisfied. Nature had decided to torment this woman by causing her to fall in love (that succession of febrile interviews, searches, feints at indifference, nightlong solitary monologues, ridiculous visions of remote happiness) with the very type of youth that could not be attracted by her, with cool impersonal learned or athletic young Northerners, a secretary at the British Embassy or Russian violinist or German archaeologist. As though these trials were not sufficient, society had added to them this aggravation, that her Roman hostesses, conscious of this failing and wishing to make sure that at their tables the Princess would display her finest flights, would intentionally include among their guests the Princess's latest infatuation to whom throughout the evening she would sing, like a swan, her song of defeated love.

As a mere girl, if I may presume to reconstruct the growth of her personality, she sensed the fact that there was in her something that a little prevented her making friends, namely, intelligence. The few intelligent people who truly wish to be liked soon learn, among the disappointments of the heart, to conceal their brilliance. They gradually convert their keen perceptions into more practical channels,—into a whole technique of implied flattery of others, into felicities of speech, into the euphemisms of demonstrative affection, into softening for others the crude lines of their dullness. All the Princess's perfection was an almost unconscious attempt at making friends of those who would first be her admirers, yet realizing that if she were too artistic they would be dazzled but repelled, and that if she were less than perfect they would dismiss her as a trivial bright hysteric. For many years she had practiced this babbling speech on her friends, unconsciously noting on their faces which tones of the voice, which appropriate fleck of the hands, which delayed adjectives were more and which less successful. In other words she had achieved mastery of a fine art, the all but forgotten art of conversation, under the impetus of love. Like some panic-stricken white mouse in the trap of a psychologist's experiment she had been seeking her ends by the primitive rules of trial and error, only to learn that at the last one is too bruised by the mistakes to enjoy the successes. The exquisite and fragile mechanism of her temperament had not been able to stand the strain laid upon it, the double exhaustion of inspiration and woe; and the lovely being was already slightly mad. She grew daily more light-headed and could be caught from time to time in moods that were variously foolish and pathetic. But her deepest wound was still to come.

James Blair and his notebooks were staying over in Rome after all. He had come upon some new veins of research. For him ten lifetimes would be all too short to pursue the horizons of one's curiosity. Think, he would say, it would take about ten years to work up the full critical apparatus to attack the historical problems surrounding the life of St. Francis of Assisi. It would take almost as many to get up the Roman road-system, the salt roads and the wheat roads,—God, the whole problem as to how the Rome of the Republic was fed. Another day he would be dreaming about starting on the eight or ten books in French and German on Christina of Sweden and her life in Rome; then one studied up Swedish and read the diaries and the barrels-full of notes; when one knew more about her than did anyone alive one passed on to her father and buried oneself for months in libraries to master the policies and the military genius of Gustavus Adolphus. Thus life stretched . . . bindings . . . bindings . . . catalogues . . . footnotes. One studied the saints and never thought about religion. One knew everything about Michelangelo yet never felt deeply a single work. James spent weeks of fascinated attention on the women of the Caesars and yet could scarcely be dragged to dinner at the Palazzo Barberini. He found all moderns trivial, and was the dupe of the historians' grand style which fails to convey the actuality (for Blair, the triviality) of their heroes. The present casts a veil of cheapness over the world: to look into any face, however beautiful, is to see pores and the folds about the eye. Only those faces not present are beautiful.

The fact is that quite early James Blair had been frightened by life (in a way which the Princess, in a moment of misery and inspiration, was to divine later with the cry: What kind of a stupid mother could he have had?) and had forever after bent upon books the floodtides of his energy. At times his scholarship resembled panic; he acted as though he feared that raising his eyes from the page he would view the world, or his share in the world, dissolving in ruin. His endless pursuit of facts (which had no fruit in published work and brought no intrinsic esthetic pleasure) was not so much the will to do something as it was the will to escape something else. One man's release lies in dreams, another's in facts.

All this resulted in a real unworldliness, which with his youth and learning and faintly *distrait* courtesy especially endeared him to older women. Both Miss Grier and Mme. Agaropoulos hovered about him with mothering delight and sighed with vexation at his obstinate refusal to come and see them. He reminded me of the lions that stare, unwinking and unseeing, at the crowd about their cage, the crowd that grimaces and waves admiring parasols, though the beast disdains to pick up even a biscuit from such vulgar givers.

At the time that the Princess's story begins he was engaged in establishing the exact location of the ancient cities of Italy. He was reading mediaeval descriptions of the Campagna and tracing through place-names, through dried water-courses, through cracked old paintings the exact position of disused roads and abandoned towns. He was learning about the country's former plants and animals: he was quite happy. Sometimes he made notes of all this, but for the most part he preferred to learn the truth and then forget it.

When it began to get cold in his room he serenely made use of mine, covering my tables with his vellum-bound folios, standing his pictures against my wall, and strewing my floors with his maps. He had dazzled one of the librarians at the Collegio Romano with his allusions and had obtained the privilege of bringing the material home.

One day the Princess d'Espoli came to see me. Ottima admitted her. She came in upon James Blair who was kneeling on the floor crawling from city to city on some yellow crested maps. His coat was off; his hair was in a tangle, and his hands were gray with dust. He had never met her and did not like her clothes. He did not want to be drawn into a conversation and stood, handsome and sulky, his glances stealing to the maps on the floor. Explained that I was out. Might not be back before. Would not forget to tell that.

Alix didn't mind. She even asked for some tea.

Ottima had just come in to begin thinking about dinner. While tea was making Alix asked to have the maps explained to her. Now the Princess was more capable of entering into an enthusiasm for old cities than most of the several hundred women of her acquaintance; but short of a doctorate in archaeology one does not enter upon such ground with James Blair. Coldly, haughtily, and with long quotations from Livy and Virgil, he harangued my guest. He dragged her remorselessly up and down the seven hills; he wrung her in and out of all the shifting beds of the Tiber. When I finally returned I found her sitting gazing at him over the edge of her teacup with a faintly mocking expression. She had not known that such a man was possible. Throughout the whole episode Blair had acted like nothing so much as a spoiled boy of seven interrupted in a game about Indians. It would be hard to say what had most captivated the Princess, but it was probably that trace of sturdy spoiled egotism. It might have been, in part, the cold douche of being unwelcome,—she who was the delight of the most delightful people in Europe, who had never entered a door without arousing a whirlpool of welcome, who had never come too early nor left too late,—suddenly she had tasted the luxury of being resented.

As soon as I arrived Blair took a swift and awkward departure.

But he's charming! He's charming! she cried. Who is he?

I told her briefly of his home, his progress through the universities, and his habits of study.

But he's extraordinary. Tell me: is he—shy, is he *boudeur* with everybody? Now perhaps I did something to annoy him? What could I have said, Samuele?

I hastened to reassure her. He's that way with everyone. And most people like him all the more for it. Especially older women. For example, Miss Grier and Mme. Agaropoulos adore him and all he does is to sit on their chairs inventing excuses for not coming to dinner.

Well, I'm not old and I like him. Oh, he is so rude! I could have slapped him. And he only looked at me once. He will have a hard time in life, Samuele, unless he learns to be more gracious. Isn't there anybody he likes, no? besides you?

Yes, he's engaged to a girl in the United States.

Dark hair or light?

I don't know.

Mark my words, he will be very unhappy, unless he learns to be more amiable. But think! what intelligence, what an eye! And how wonderful it is to see such an absence of trickery, you know, such simplicity. Does he live here?

No, he just brings his books in here when it's too cold in his own room.

He is poor?

Yes.

He is poor!

Not very poor, you know. When he really gets down to his last cent he can always find things to do at once. He's happy to be poor.

And he lives quite alone?

Yes. Oh, yes.

And he is poor. (This caused her a moment's astonished reflection, until she burst out:) But you know, that is not right! It is society's duty . . . that is, society should be proud to protect such people. Someone very gifted should be appointed to watch over such people.

But, Princess, James Blair values his independence above everything. He doesn't want to be watched over.

They should be watched over in spite of themselves. Look, you will bring him to tea some day. I am sure my husband's library has

some more old maps of the Campagna. We have the bailiff's reports of the Espoli back into the Sixteenth Century. Wouldn't that
bring him?

Even surprised at herself, the Princess tried for a time to talk of
other things, but presently she returned to praise what she called
Blair's single-mindedness; she meant his self-sufficiency, for while
we are in love with a person our knowledge of his weaknesses lies
lurking in the back of our minds and our idealization of the loved
one is not so much an exaggeration of his excellences as a careful
"rationalization" of his defects.

When next I saw Blair he wasted two or three hours before he
got up courage to ask me who she was. He listened darkly while I
spoke my enthusiasm. At last he showed me a note in which she
asked him to drive with her to Espoli, look over the estate, and to
examine the archives. He was to bring me if I wanted. James
wished greatly to go; but he was suspicious of the lady. He liked
her and yet he didn't. He was trying to tell me that he only liked
ladies who didn't like him first. He twisted the letter about trying
to decide, then going to the table wrote a note of refusal.

Then began what it is merely brutal to call a siege. Driving in
the Corso Alix would say to herself: There's nothing unconven-
tional in my stopping at his room to see if he wants to drive in the
Gardens. I could do as much for a dozen men and it would be
perfectly natural. I am much older than he is, so much so, that it
would merely be an act of . . . thoughtfulness. When she stood
on the platform before his door (for she was not content to send
up the chauffeur) she would experience a moment of panic,
wishing to recall her ring, imagining when no one answered that
he was in hiding behind the closed door, listening, who knows, in
anger or contempt to her loud heartbeats. Or she would debate all
evening among the gilt chairs of her little salon as to whether she

might drop him a note. She would count the days since last she had spoken to him and gauge the propriety (the inner, the spiritual propriety, not the worldly propriety: for the Cabalists the latter had ceased to exist) of a new meeting. She was always coming upon him by accident in the city (she called it her proof of the existence of guardian angels) and it was with these chance meetings that she had generally to content herself. She would attract his attention the length of the Piazza Venezia and carry him to whatever destination he confessed to. No one has ever been happier than Alix on these few occasions when she sat beside him in her car. How docilely she sat listening to his lecture; with what tenderness she secretly noticed his tie and shoes and socks: and with what intensity she fixed her gaze upon his face trying to imprint upon her memory the exact proportions of his features, the imprint that indifference retains so much better than the most passionate love. There was a possibility that they might have become the most congenial of friends, for he dimly sensed that there was something in her that allied her to the great ladies of his study. If she had only succeeded in concealing her tenderness. At the first signs of his liking for her she would become so intoxicated with the intimation of cordiality that she would make some shy little remark with a faintly senti-mental implication; she would comment on his appearance or ask him to lunch. And lose him.

One day he gave her a book that had been mentioned in their conversations. He did not stop to think that it was the first move he had made spontaneously in the whole relation. Hitherto every suggestion, every invitation, had proceeded from her (from her, trembling, presuffering a rebuff, lightly) and she longed for a first sign of his interest. When this book was brought to her, then, she lost her balance; she thought it justified her in pushing the friend-ship on to new levels, to almost daily meetings, and to long comradely lazy afternoons. She never realized that in his eyes she was, first, an enemy to his studies, and second, that strange hedged monster which all his wide reading had not been able to humanize: a married woman. She called once too often. Suddenly he changed; he became rude and abrupt. When she climbed his stairs he *did* hide behind the door and the bell rang in vain and with a menacing sound, though she had her ways of knowing he was in. She became terrified. Again she confronted that cavern of horror in her nature: she seemed always to be loving those that did not love her. She came to me, distraught. I was cautious and offered her philosophy until I could sound Blair in the matter.

Blair came to me of his own accord. He paced up and down the room, bewildered, revolted, enraged. His stay in Rome had become impossible. He no longer dared remain in his room and when he was out he clung to the side streets. What should he do?

I advised him to leave town.

But how could he? He was in the middle of some work that. Some work that. Damn it all. All right, he'd go.

I begged him before he went to come to dinner with me once when the Princess would be present. No, no. Anything but that. I, in turn, became angry. I analyzed the different kinds of fool he was. An hour later I was saying that the mere fact of being loved so, whether one could return it or not, put one under an obligation. More than an obligation to be merely kind, an obligation to be grateful. Blair did not understand, but consented at last on the difficult condition that I was not to reveal to the Princess that he was leaving for Spain on the very night of the dinner.

Of course, the Princess arrived early, so enchantingly dressed that I fairly floundered in admitting her. She held tickets for the opera; one no longer cared to hear *Salome,* but *Petrushka* was being danced after it, at ten-thirty. Blair's train left at eleven. He arrived and played his most gracious. We were really very happy, all of us, as we sat by the open window, smoking and talking long over Ottima's excellent *zabaglione* and harsh Trasteverine coffee.

It was a continual surprise to me to see that in Blair's presence she was always a proud detached aristocrat. Even her faintly caressing remarks were such as would not be noticed if one had let them fall to someone with whom one was not secretly in love. Her fastidious pride even drove her to exaggerating her impersonality; she teased him, she pretended she did not hear when he addressed her, she pretended she was in love with me. It was only when he was not present that she became humble, even servile; only then could she even imagine calling on him unasked. At last she rose: It's time to go to the Russian Ballet, she said.

Blair excused himself: I'm sorry I must go back and work.

She looked as though a sword had gone through her. But surely, three-quarters of an hour with Stravinsky is a part of your work. My car's right here.

He remained firm. He too had a ticket for that night.

For a moment she looked blank. She had never met obstinacy under such conditions and did not know what to do next. After a moment she bent her head and pushed back her coffee-cup. Very well, she said lightly. If you can't, you can't. Samuele and I shall go.

Their parting was grim. During the drive to the Constanzi she remained silent, fingering the folds of her coat; during the ballet she sat at the back of the box thinking, thinking, thinking, with staring dry eyes. At the close scores of friends pressed about her in the corridor. She became gay: Let's go to the cabaret run by the Russian refugees, she said. At the door of the cabaret she dismissed her chauffeur, telling him that her maid need not sit up for her. We danced for a long time in silence, her depression stealing back upon her.

When we left the hall the unfriendliest moonlight in the world was flooding the street. We found a carriage and started towards her home. But falling into the most earnest conversation in all our acquaintance we failed to notice that the carriage had reached her door and had been standing there for some time.

Look, Samuele, do not make me go to bed now. Let me go in and change my clothes quickly. Then let us drive about and watch the sun come up over the Campagna. Would that make you angry with me?

I assured her that it was just what I wanted and she hurried into the house. I paid off the driver who was drunk and quarrelsome and when she rejoined me we strolled through the streets talking and gradually inviting a resigned drowsiness. We had experimented with vodka at the cabaret and the alcohol conferred upon our minds the same mood that the moonlight was shedding upon the icy bubble of the Pantheon. We strayed into the courtyard of the Cancelleria and criticized the arches. We returned to my rooms for cigarettes.

Last night I wasn't at all brave, she said, lying back in the darkness on the sofa. I was desperate. That was before I received your invitation. Could I go to see him or couldn't I? A week had gone by. I asked myself would he feel . . . well, insulted, if a lady knocked on his door at ten o'clock. It was about ten o'clock. Really, there's nothing peculiar about a lady's paying a perfectly impersonal call at about nine-thirty. There's nothing self-conscious, Samuele, about my being here now, for instance. Besides I had a perfectly good reason for going. He asked me what I thought of La Villegiatura, and since then I had read it. Now tell, my dear friend, would it have been ridiculous from the American point of view if I had . . . ?

Beautiful Alix, you are never ridiculous. But wasn't your meeting with him tonight all the fresher, all the happier, just because you hadn't seen him for so long?

Oh, how wise you are! she cried. God has sent you to me in my trouble. Come by me and let me hold your hand. Are you ashamed of me when you have seen me suffer so? I suppose I should be ashamed. You see me without any dignity. You have kind eyes and I am not ashamed in front of you. I think you must have loved too, for you take all my foolishness as a matter of course. Oh, my dear Samuele, every now and then the thought comes over me that he despises me. I have all the faults that he hasn't. When I have this nightmare that he not only dislikes me but laughs at me, yes, laughs at me, my heart stops beating and I blush for hours at a time. The only way I can save myself then is by remembering that he has said many kind things to me; that he sent me that book; that he has asked after me. And then I pray God very simply to put into his mind just a bit of regard for me. Just a bit of respect for those things . . . those things that other people seem to like in me.

We sat in silence for a time, her feverish hand plunged deep into mine and her bright eyes gazing into the darkness. At last she began speaking again in a lower voice:

He is good. He is reasonable. When I am analytical this way I unfit myself for his loving me. I must learn to be simple. Yes. Look, you have done so much for me, may I ask for one more favor. Play to me. I must get out of my mind that wonderful music where Petrushka wrestles with himself.

I felt ashamed of playing before her who played far better than any of us, but I drew out my folios and started right through Gluck's *Armide*. I had hoped that the inept performance would awaken an esthetic annoyance and so shake her out of her dejection, but I presently saw that she had fallen asleep. After a long and adroit diminuendo I left the piano, turned on a shaded light

near her, and stole off into my own room. I changed my clothes
and lay down ready for the walk in which we were to see the sun
rise. I was trembling with a strange happy excitement, made up
partly of my love and pity for her, and partly from the mere
experience of eavesdropping on a beautiful spirit in the last reaches
of its pride and suffering. I was lying thus, proud and happy in the
role of guardian, when my heart suddenly stopped beating. She
was weeping in her sleep. Sighs welled up from the depths of her
slumber, hoarse protests, obstinate denials and moans followed
one upon another. Suddenly her broken breathing ceased and I
knew she was awake. There was a half-minute of silence; then a
low call: Samuele.

Hardly had I appeared at the door before she cried: I know he
despises me. He runs away from me. He thinks me a foolish
woman who pursues him. He tells the servant to tell me he is out,
but he stands behind the door and hears me go away. What shall I
do? I'd better not live. I'd better not live any more. It's best, dear
Samuele, that I go out right now, in my own way, and stop all this
mistaken, this, this, futile suffering of mine. Do you see?

She had arisen and was groping for her hat. I really have
courage enough tonight, she muttered. He is too good and too
simple for me to worry him as I do. I'll just slip out . . .

But Alix, I cried. We love you so. So many people love you.

You can't say that people love me. They like to greet me on the
stairs. They like to listen and smile. But no one has ever watched
under my window. No one has secretly learned what I do every
hour of the day. No one has . . .

She lay back on the sofa, her cheeks flushed and wet. I talked to
her for a long time. I said that her genius was social, that she was
made for the delight of company, that she relieved others of the
weight of their own boredom, their disguised self-hatred. I prom-

ised her that she could find happiness in the exercise of her gift. I could see by a glimpse of her wet cheek turned away that it calmed her to be told so, for she possessed the one form of genius that is almost never praised to its face. She grew more tranquil. After a pause she began talking in a dreamy tone:

I will leave him alone. I will never see him again, she began. When I was a girl and we lived on the mountains, Samuele, I had a pet goat named Tertullien that I loved very much. One day Tertullien died. I would not be comforted. I was hateful and obstinate. The nuns with whom I went to school could do nothing with me and when it was my turn to recite I refused to speak. At last my dear Mother Superior called me into her room and at first I was very bad, even with her. But when she began to tell me of her losses I flung my arms about her and wept for the first time. As a punishment she made me stop everyone I met and say to them twice: *God is sufficient! God is sufficient!*

After a pause she added: I know that it can be true for other people, but I still wanted Tertullien. When is your patience with me coming to an end, Samuele?

Never, I said.

The windows were beginning to show the first light of dawn. Suddenly a little bell rang out nearby, a tinkle of purest silver.

Hush, she said. That's the earliest mass at some church.

Santa Maria in Trastevere is just around the corner.

Hurry!

We let ourselves out of the palace and breathed the cold gray air. A mist seemed to hang low about the street; puffs of blue smoke lay in the corners. A cat passed us. Shivering but elated we entered the church joining two old women in wadded clothes and a laborer. The basilica loomed above, the candles of our side-chapel picking out reflections in the curious marbles and the gold of the

mosaics in the vast black cave. The service of the Mass was en-
rolled with expedition and accuracy. When we came out a milky
light had begun to fill the square. The shutters of several shops
were being lowered; drowsy passers-by made the diagonals
staggering; a woman was lowering her chickens in a basket from
the fifth story for a long day's scratching.

We walked over to the Aventine, crossing the Tiber which
twisted like a great yellow rope under a delicate fume. We stopped
for a glass of sour blue-black wine and a paper bag of peaches.

For the time at least the Princess seemed to herself to have forever closed her mind to even the remotest hope that she would ever
see Blair again. Sitting on a stone bench on the gloomy Aventine
while the sun shouldered its way up through plunging orange
clouds, we mused. She seemed for a time to have fallen back into
her old despondency; I resumed the arguments that spoke more
glowingly of her gifts.

Suddenly she straightened up. All right. I will try it for you. I
must do something. Where are you going today?

I murmured that Mme. Agaropoulos was giving a sort of a
musicale: that she was introducing a young compatriot who
claimed to have discovered the secret of ancient Greek music.

Write her a note. Telephone her. Ask her if I may come. I too
shall learn about ancient Greek music. I shall be introduced to
everyone there. I shall be asked to everyone's house. Listen,
Samuele, since you say it is my talent I shall get to know everyone
in Rome. I shall die of social engagements: Here lies the woman
who never refused an invitation. I shall meet two thousand people
in ten days. I shall lay myself out to please anybody on earth. And
mind you, Samuele, if that does not nourish me, we shall have to
finish trying, you know. . . .

Mme. Agaropoulos was staggered with joy when she discovered

that the unhoped for, the improcurable Princess was coming to her house. Mme. Agaropoulos was not the slave of social categories, but she longed to frequent the Cabala, as some long for the next world. She assumed that in that company all was wit and love and peace. There one would find no silly people, none envious, none quarrelsome. She had met the Princess d'Espoli once and had ever since taken her as the type of person she would herself have been if she had been better-looking, thinner and had had more time to read, little realizing that all these had been more in her power than in Alix', and that she had spoiled her own progress by a lazy kindliness, great kindliness but lazy.

The Princess called for me in her car at five o'clock. It would be impossible for me to describe her clothes; it is enough to say that she had the most incredible power of supplying new angles, shades, lines, that interpreted her character. This aptitude received added éclat from her residence in Italy, for Italian women, though often more beautiful, lack both figure and judgment. They anxiously spend enormous sums in Paris and achieve nothing but bundles of rich stuffs that bulge or trail or blow about them in effects they half guess to be unsuccessful, and seek to repair with a display of stones.

We pursued the Via Po for a mile or two and alighted at the ugliest of its houses, an example of that modern German architecture that has done so much for factories. As we mounted the stairs she kept muttering: Watch me! Watch me! In the hall we found a host of latecomers standing with their fingers on their lip while from the drawing rooms there issued the sound of passionate declamation accompanied by the plucking of a lyre, the desolate *moto perpetuo* of an oriental flute and a rhythmic clapping of hands. In other words we had arrived too early; our campaign for meeting two thousand souls in ten days was being balked at the outset. Fretted we pushed on into the garden behind the house. Sitting down on a stone bench, with the tragic ode still faintly sounding in our ears we gave our attention to the spectacle in the middle distance of a white-haired gentleman in a wheel-chair overflowing with brightly-colored shawls. This was Jean Perraye; I told the Princess of how Mme. Agaropoulos had found the saintly old French poet at the point of death, wrapt in shawls in a wretched little hotel at Pisa, and how by supplying him with tender interest, whole milk and a group of pet animals she had restored his muse, comforted his last years and effected his entrance into the French Academy. At this moment he was engaged in addressing a circle of attentive cats. These six cats, intermittently licking the fine silk of their shoulders, and casting polite glances at their patron, were gray angoras, the color of cigarette ash. We had read the poet's latest book and knew their names: six queens of France. We practically dozed on the bench—the hot sunlight, the choruses of the *Antigone* behind and Jean Perraye's exordium to the queens of France and Persia before, would have made drowsy even those who had not passed a night of confession and tears.

When we came to ourselves the audition was over and the company, doubly noisy after music, was shouting its appreciation. We re-entered the house, hungry for pastry and encounters. A sea of hats, with scores of self-conscious eyes staring about in perpetual search of new salutations, marking down the Princess for their own; occasionally the large stomach of a senator or an ambassador swathed in serge and bound with a golden chain.

Who's the lady in the black hat? whispered Alix.

Signora Daveni, the great engineer's wife.

Fancy! Will you bring her to me or should you take me to her. No, I'll go to her. Take me.

Signora Daveni was a plain little woman presenting the high

lifted forehead and fresh eyes of an idealistic boy. Her husband
was one of Italy's foremost engineers, an inventor of many tre-
mendous trifles in airplane construction and a bulwark of conservative methods in the rising storm of labor agitation. The Signora
was on every philanthropic committee of any importance in the
whole country and during the War had directed incalculable
labors. The consciousness of her responsibilities combined with a
touch of brusqueness from her humble extraction had brought her
into many a short triumphant struggle with cabinets and senates
and there are stories of her having sharply rebuked the vague, well-
intentioned interferences of the royal ladies of Savoy. Yet these
distinctions had only made her manners the simpler and her quick
cordiality was continually deflating the deference that was paid to
her. She dressed badly; she walked badly, her large feet pushing
before her like those of some jar-carrier in an upland village. It had
been rather fine in uniform, but now that she must return to hats
and gowns and rings the consciousness of her lack of grace caused
her much depression. Her home was in Turin, but she lived a great
deal in Rome out among the open lots of the Via Nomentana and
knew everyone. The Princess with the unexpectedness that lies in
the very definition of genius turned the conversation upon the use
of sphagnum moss as a surgical dressing. The diverse excellence of
the two women glimpsed one another; the Princess was astonished
to find such quiet mastery in a woman without a *de* and the
Signora was amazed to find the same quality in a noblewoman.

I drifted off, but presently the Princess rejoined me. She is real,
that woman. I am going to dinner with her Friday; so are you.
Find me some more. Who is that blonde with the voice?

You don't want to know her, Princess.

She must be important with that voice; who is she?

She is the woman in the whole world who is most your opposite.

Then I must know her. Will she give me tea and introduce me to a dozen people?

Oh, yes, she'll do that. But you haven't a thing in common. She is a narrow British woman, Princess. Her only interest is in the Protestant Church. She lives in a little British hotel. . . .

But where does she get that *authority*—and the Princess made a gesture of perfect mimicry.

Well, I admitted, she has received the highest honors an Englishwoman can receive. She wrote a hymn and they made her a Dame of the British Empire.

You see I must be caught out of myself. I must meet her right now.

So I led her up to Dame Edith Steuert, Mrs. Edith Foster Prichard Steuert, author of "Far From Thy Ways, I Strayed," the greatest hymn since Newman's. Daughter, wife, sister, what not, of clergymen, she lived in the most exciting currents of Anglicanism. Her conversation ran on vacant livings and promising young men from Shropshire, and on the editorials in the latest *St. George's Banner* and *The Anglican Cry*. She sat on platforms and raised subscriptions and got names. She seemed to be forever surrounded by a ballet of curates and widows who, at her word, rose and swayed and passed the scones. For she was the author of the greatest hymn of modern times and gazing at her one wondered when the mood could have struck this loud conceited woman, the mood that had prompted those eight verses of despair and humility. The hymn could have been written by Cowper, that gentle soul exposed to the flame of an evangelism too hot even for Negroes. For one minute in her troubled girlhood all the intermittent sincerity of generations of clergymen must have combined in her, and late at night, full of dejections she could not understand, she must have committed to her diary that heartbroken confession. Then the fit was over, and over for ever. It was a telling example of that great mystery in religious and artistic experience: the occasional profundity of nobodies. Dame Edith Steuert on being presented, straightened visibly to show that she was not impressed by the title. With a candor that was another surprise, Alix asked her if she might use her name as reference on her nephew's application for entrance into Eton College. To be sure the nephew was in Lyons, but if Dame Edith would permit the Princess to call upon her some afternoon she would bring some of the boy's letters, photographs and sufficient apparatus to convince her that he was a student recommendable. Friday afternoon was agreed upon, and the Princess rejoined me for new introductions.

So it went on for an hour. The Princess had no method; each new encounter was a new problem. Within three minutes the meeting became an acquaintance, and the acquaintance a friendship. Little did the new friends guess how strange it was to her. She kept asking me what their husbands "did." It delighted her to think that their husbands did anything; she had never guessed that one could meet such people and smiled amazedly like a girl about to meet a real printed poet. A doctor's wife, the wife of a man in rubber, fancy. . . . Toward the end of the afternoon her enthusiasm waned. I feel a little dusty, she whispered. I feel very Bovary. To think that all this has been going on in Rome without my knowing it. I'll go and say goodbye to Mme. Agaropoulos,—*tiens,* who is that beautiful lady. That is an American, isn't it? Quick.

For the only time in my life I saw the beautiful and unhappy Mrs. Darrell who had come to take leave of her Roman friends. As she entered the room a silence fell upon the company; there was something antique, something Plato would have seized upon in the effect of her beauty. She made much of it, with that touch of conceit that we allow to a great musician listening exaggeratedly to his own perfect phrasing, or to the actor who sets aside author, fellow-players and the fable itself, in order to improvise the last excessive moments of a death scene. She dressed, she glanced, she moved and spoke as only uncontested beauties may: she too revived a lost fine art. To this virtuosity of appearing, her illness and suffering had added a quality even she could not estimate, a magic of implied melancholy. But all this perfection of hers was unapproachable; none of her dearest friends, not even Miss Morrow, dared to kiss her. She was like a statue in a solitude. She presuffered her death, and her spirit was set in defiance. She hated every atom of a creation where such things were possible. The next week she was to retire to her villa at Capri with her collection of Mantegnas and Bellinis and to live through four months with their treacherous love-affair and to die. But this day in the serenity of the selfishness that was her perfection and the selfishness that was her illness she effaced the room.

He would have loved me if I had looked like that, breathed Alix into my ear, and sinking into a retired chair covered her mouth with her hand.

Mme. Agaropoulos took Helen Darrell's fingertips a little timidly and led her to the finest chair. No one seemed able to say anything. Luigi and Vittorio, sons of the house, went up and kissed her hand; the American ambassador approached to compliment her.

She is beautiful. She is beautiful, muttered Alix to herself. The world is hers. She will never have to suffer as I must. She is beautiful.

It would not have consoled the Princess if I had explained to her that Helen Darrell, having been admired extravagantly from the cradle, had never been obliged to cultivate her intelligence to retain her friends and that, if I may say it respectfully, her mind was still that of a school-girl.

Fortunately the flautist was still there to play and during the performance of the Paradise music from Orpheus scarcely a pair of eyes in the room left the newcomer's face. She sat perfectly straight, allowing herself none of the becoming attitudes which music suggests to her kind, no ardent attention, no starry-eyed revery. I remember thinking she marked too deliberately the anti-sentimental. When the music was over she asked to be taken to say goodbye, for the present, to Jean Perraye. From the window I could see them alone together, with the gray cats, queens of France, moving meaninglessly about them. One wonders what they said to one another as she knelt beside his chair: as he said later, they loved one another because they were ill.

Alix d'Espoli would not stir until she knew that Mrs. Darrell had left the house and garden. All her suffering had rushed back upon her. She pretended to be sipping a cup of tea while she gathered herself together. I understand now, she murmured hoarsely. God has never meant me to be happy. Others may be happy with one another. But I shall never be. I know that now. Let us go.

Then began what was ever after known to the Cabala as Alix aux Enfers. She would lunch at a tiny pension with some English spinsters; stop in at some studio in the Via Margutta; pass through a reception at an Embassy; dance till seven at the Hotel Russie as the guest of some cosmetic manufacturer's wife; dine with the Queen Mother; hear the last two acts of the Opera in Marconi's box. Even after that she might feel the need of finishing the day at the Russian cabaret, perhaps contributing herself a monologue to the program. She no longer had any time to see the Cabala and it watched her progress with terror. They begged her to come back to

them, but she only laughed at them with her bright febrile eyes
and dashed off into her new-found whirlpools. Long after when
some Roman name arose in their conversation they would all cry:
Alix knows them! To which she would reply coolly: Of course I
know them, and a roar would arise from the table. The acquaintances she was now pursuing for distraction, I had long since
pursued for study or from simple liking; but she soon outstripped
me by the hundreds. I went to a few engagements with her, but
often enough we would come upon one another in ludicrous
situations; whereupon we would retire behind a door and compare
notes as to how we got there. Did Commendatore Boni ask a few
people to the Palatine? she was there. Did Benedetto Croce give a
private reading of a paper on George Sand? we glimpsed one
another gravely in that solemn air. She lost a comb in defense of
Reality at the stormy opening of Pirandello's *Sei Personaggi in
Cerca d'Autore;* at Casella's party for Mengelberg, who had been
surpassing himself at the Augusteo, dear old Bossi stood on her
train and the sound of ripping satin caught the enraptured ear of a
dozen organists.

When the bourgeoisie discovered that she was accepting invitations there was a tumult as of many waters. Most of her hostesses
assumed that she would not have come to them were it not for the
fact that better doors were beginning to be closed against her, but
fair or foul they would accept her. And they had her at her best;
the faint touch of frenzy that was driving her on only rendered her
gift the more dazzling. People who had spent their lives laughing
at tiresome jokes were now given something to laugh at. She
would be begged to do this or that "bit" which had become
famous. Have you heard Alix do the Talking Horse? No, but she
did the Kronprinz in Frascati for us last Friday. Oh, aren't you
lucky!

For the first time she was seeing something of artists and among them she was enjoying her liveliest successes. The underpainting of her misery which especially these days rendered her wit so magical was much clearer to them than to the manufacturers. They never failed to mention it and their love led them to paying her the strangest tributes which at the time she was in too great a daze to stop and value.

For a while I thought she was enjoying all this. She would laugh so naturally over some of the accidents of the days. Moreover I noticed that she was forming some very rare attachments and I hoped that the friendship of Signora Daveni or of Duse or of Besnard would be able to comfort and finally reconcile her. But one evening I was suddenly shown how utterly ineffectual this plunging about the jungle was.

After a month's absence James Blair wrote me from Spain that he had to come back to Rome, even if it were only for a week. He promised to see no one, to keep up side streets and to get out as soon as it was possible.

I wrote him back in the strongest profanity that it was impossible. Go anywhere else. Don't fool with such things.

He replied, no less angry, that he could move about the earth as freely as everybody else. Whether I liked it or not he was coming to Rome the following Wednesday and nothing would stop him. He was on the traces of the Alchemists. He wanted to know all that was left of the old secret societies and his search was leading to Rome. Since I could do nothing to prevent his coming I could at least devote my energies to concealing it. I took almost ridiculous precautions. I even saw to it that Mlle. de Morfontaine had Alix in Tivoli over the week-end and that Besnard had her sitting for a portrait most of the mornings. But there is a certain spiritual law that requires our tragic coincidences. Which of us has not felt it? Take no precautions.

The seer whom Blair had returned to visit, Sareptor Basilis, lived in three rooms on the top floor of an old palace in the Via Fontanella di Borghese. Rumor had it that he could make lightning play about his left hand and that when his meditations approached ecstasy he could be seen sitting among the broken arcs of a dozen rainbows; and that as you mounted the dark stairs you fought your way through the welcoming ghosts as through a swarm of bees. In the front room where the meetings were held (Wednesdays for adepts, Saturdays for beginners) one was awed by discovering a circular hole in the roof that was never closed. Under it had been laid a zinc-lined depression that carried off the rain water and in this depression stood the master's chair.

Long meditation and ecstatic trances had certainly beautified his face. His blue-green eyes, not incapable of sudden acuteness, drifted vaguely about under a smooth pink forehead; he had the bushy white eyebrows and beard of Blake's Creator. Except for his long walks he seemed to have no private life, but sat all day and night under the hole in the roof, lending an ear to a whispering visitor, writing slowly with his left hand, or gazing up into the sky. A host of people from every walk of life sought him out and held him in reverence. He gave no thought to practical necessities, for his admirers, spiritually prompted, were continually leaving significant looking envelopes beside him on the zinc-lined depression. Some left bottles of wine and bars of bread, and brown silk shirts. The only human occupation that arrested his attention was music, and it is said that he would stand by the door of the Augusteo on the afternoon of a symphony concert and wait for some passerby, spiritually prompted, to buy him a ticket. If none came, he would continue on his way without bitterness. He composed music himself, hymns for unaccompanied voices which he affirmed he had heard in dream. They were written in a notation resembling our own, but not sufficiently so to allow of transcription. I have puzzled for hours over the score of a certain *Lo, where the rose of dispersion empurples the dawn.* This motet for ten voices, a chorus of angels on the last day, began plainly enough with the treble clef on five staves, but how was one to interpret a sudden shrinkage of the horizontal lines to two in all parts? I humbly approached the master on this subject. He replied that the effect of the music at that point could only be expressed by a radical departure from standard notation; that the economy of staves denoted an acuity of pitch; that the note on which my thumb was reposing was an E, a violet E, an E of the quality of a lately-warmed amethyst . . . music powerless to express . . . ah . . . the rose of dispersion empurples. At first the nonsense in which he moved and thought enraged me. I invented opportunities for provoking his absurdity. I improvised a story about a pilgrim who had come up to me in the nave of the Lateran and told me it was God's will that I should return with him to a leper colony in Australia. Dear Master, I cried, how shall I know if this be my real vocation? His answer was not clear. I was told that destiny herself was the mother of decision, and that my vocation would be settled by events not by consideration. In the next breath I was bidden to do nothing rashly; to lay my ear over the lute of eternity and to plan my life in harmony with the cosmic overtones. During the course of a year thousands of women visited him, of every rank, and in every sort of perplexity, and to each one he offered the comforts of metaphor. They came away from him with shining faces; these phrases were beautiful and profound to them; they wrote them in their diaries and murmured them over to themselves when they were tired.

Basilis was attended by two homely sisters, the Adolfini girls. Lise must have been thirty and Vanna about twenty-eight. They say that he ran across them in the Italian quarter of London where

they were serving as attendants in a ballet school. Penury and
abuse had left them scarcely the human semblance. Every evening
at eleven when they had unlaced the last slipper of the night class,
treated the floor with tallow, polished the bars and tied up the
chandelier, they went around the corner to the Café Roma for a
thimbleful of coffee to sip with their bread. Here Basilis was to be
found, a photographer's assistant with grandiose pretensions. He
was vice-president of the Rosicrucian Mysteries, Soho Chapter, a
group of clerks, waiters and idealistic barbers who found compensation for the humiliations they underwent by day in the glories
they ascribed to themselves by night. They met in darkened rooms,
took oaths with one hand resting on the works of Swedenborg,
read papers on the fabrication of gold and its metaphysical impli-
cations, and elected one another with great earnestness to the
offices of arch-adept and *magister hieraticorum*. They corresponded
with similar societies in Birmingham, Paris and Sydney, and sent
sums of money to the last of the magi, Orzinda-Mazda of Mount
Sinai. Basilis first discovered his power over the minds of women
when he fell into the habit of talking to the two mute sisters in the
café. They listened wide-eyed to his stories of how some workmen
near Rome, breaking by chance into the tomb of Cicero's daughter,
Tulliola, discovered an ever-burning lamp suspended in mid-air,
its wick feeding on Perpetual Principle; of how Cleopatra's son
Caesarion was preserved in a translucent liquid "oil of gold," and
could be still seen in an underground shrine at Vienna; and of how
Virgil never died, but was alive still on the Island of Patmos,
eating the leaves of a peculiar tree. The wonder-stories, the nar-
rator's apocalyptic eyes, the excitement of being spoken to without
anger, and the occasional offer of Vermouth bewitched the sisters.
They became his unquestioning slaves; with the money they had
saved up he opened a Temple where his gift met extraordinary

success. The girls left the ballet school and became doorkeepers in the house of their lord. The new leisure into which they entered, the sufficient food, the privilege of serving Basilis, his confidence and his love, combined to constitute a burden of happiness almost too great to be borne. Happiness is in proportion to humility: the humility of the Adolfini girls was so profound that there was in it no room for the expression of gratitude or surprise; in the face of it food could not fatten them nor love soften their bony features; not even when after some altercation with the London police Basilis and his handmaidens removed to their native Rome. To be sure the master in turn never confessed his indebtedness to the girls for their silent and skillful ministration. Even in love he was impersonal; they merely provided him with that mood of gentle satiety of the senses which is an indispensable element of the philosopher's meditation.

It was under this skylight then that Blair and I sat at about eleven-thirty, waiting for the public séance to begin. We were early, and leaning back against the wall we watched the little group of visitors that one by one moved up to the unboxed confessional that was the master's ear. A clerk with watery eyes and trembling hands; a stout lady of the middle class, gripping a large shopping purse and talking with great rapidity about her *nepote;* a trim little professional woman, probably a lady's maid, stuffing a tiny handkerchief into her mouth as she sobbed. Basilis' eyes seldom strayed to his vistors' faces; while he dismissed them with a few measured grave sentences his glance revealed nothing but its serene abstraction. Presently a younger woman, heavily veiled, crossed the floor swiftly to the empty chair beside him. She must have been there before, for she lost no time in greetings. Under deep emotion she pleaded with him. A little surprised by her vehemence he interrupted her several times with the words *Mia figlia.* The reproaches only increased her energy, and brushing back her veil with her hand in order to thrust her face into the sage's she revealed herself as Alix d'Espoli. Terror went through me; I seized Blair's arm and made signs that we were to escape. But at that moment the Princess with a gesture of anger, as though she had come, not so much to ask the sage's counsel, as to announce a determination, rose and turned to the door. Unerringly her eyes met ours, and the rebellious light died out, to be replaced by fear. For a moment the three of us hung suspended on one cord of horror. Then the Princess collected herself long enough to tincture the despairing contraction of her mouth with a smile; she bowed to us deliberately in turn and passed almost majestically from the room.

At once I returned home and wrote her a long letter, using the whole truth as a surgeon in an extremity would resort to a wholesale guesswork with the knife. I never received an answer. And our friendship was over. I had often to meet her again, and we even came finally to have agreeable conversations together, but we never mentioned the affair and there was a glaze of impersonality over her eyes.

From the night she had seen us in Basilis' rooms the Princess gave up her social researches as abruptly as she had begun them. Nor did she ever go to the Rosicrucian again. I heard that she was attempting the few remaining consolations that lie open to affliction: she took to the fine arts; she climbed up ladders respectfully placed for her in the Sistine Chapel and stared at the frescos through magnifying glasses; she resumed the culture of her voice and even sang a little in public. She started off on a trip to Greece, but came back without any explanations a week later. There was a hospital phase during which she cut off her hair and tiptoed about among the wards.

At last the beating of the wings, the darting about the cage, subsided. She had come to the second stage of convalescence: the mental pain that had been so great that it had to be passed into the physical and that expressed itself in movement, had now sufficiently abated to permit her to think. All her vivacity left her and she sat about in her friends' homes listening to their visitors.

Little by little then her old graces began to reappear. First a few wry sarcasms, gently slipping off her tongue; then some rueful narratives in which she appeared in a poor light; then ever so gradually the wit, the energy, and last of all the humor.

The whole Cabala trembled with joy, but pretended to have noticed nothing. Only one night when for the first time at table she had returned to her gorgeous habit of teasing the Cardinal on his Chinese habits, only once on leaving the table did he take her two hands and gaze deep into her eyes with a significant smile that both reproached her for her long absence and welcomed her back. She blushed slightly and kissed the sapphire.

I, who know nothing about such things, assumed that the grand passion was over and dreaded any moment seeing her interesting herself in some new Northerner. But one little incident taught me how deep a wound may be.

One afternoon at the villa in Tivoli we were standing on the balcony overlooking the falls. Whenever she was left alone with me her charm abated; she seemed to be fearing that I might attempt a confidence; the muscles at the corners of her mouth would tighten. We were joined from the house by a well-known Danish archaeologist who began to discourse upon the waterfall and its classical associations. Suddenly he stopped and turning to me, cried:

Oh, I have a message for you. How could I have forgotten that! I met a friend of yours in Paris. A young American named Blair— let me see, was it Blair?

Yes, Doctor.

What a young man! How many of you Americans are like that? I suppose you never met him, Princess? . . .

Yes, replied Alix, I knew him too.

Such intelligence! He is surely the greatest instinctive scholar I have ever met, and, believe me, perhaps he is all the greater for never putting anything down on paper. And such modesty, Princess,—the modesty of the great scholar that knows that all the learning one human head can hold is but a grain of dust. I spent two whole nights over his notebooks and I honestly felt as though I had brushed against a Leonardo, really, a Leonardo.

We both stood rapt, listening to the waves of happy praise when suddenly I became aware that the Princess had fainted beside me with a happy smile upon her face.

BOOK FOUR

ASTRÉE-LUCE AND THE CARDINAL

There was a vague understanding among the members of the Cabala that I was engaged upon the composition of a play about Saint Augustine. None of my friends had ever seen the manuscript (even I was surprised to come upon it every now and then at the bottom of my trunk), but it was treated with enormous respect. Mlle. de Morfontaine especially kept asking about it, kept walking about on tiptoes and glancing at it sideways. It was to this that she was alluding in the note I received soon after Blair's frightened departure: Try and arrange to come up to the Villa for a few weeks. It is perfectly quiet until five o'clock every afternoon. You can work on your poem.

It was my turn for a little peace. I had so recently passed through the desperations of Marcantonio and Alix. I sat holding the note for a long while, my wary nervous system begging me to be cautious, begging me to make sure that no hysterical evenings could possibly lie behind it. Here was a place where it was perfectly quiet until five o'clock every afternoon. It was five o'clock every morning that I wanted to be reassured about. You can work

on your poem. Surely the only vexation that could proceed from
that wonderful lady lay exactly there,—she would be asking me
every morning about the progress on the Third Act. It would be
good for me to be hectored about my play. And what wonderful
wines she stored. To be sure the lady was mad, indubitably mad.
But mad in a nice way, with perfect dignity; decently mad on a
million a year. I wrote her I would come.

What could have been more reassuring than the first days?
Mornings of sunlight when the dust settled thicker on the olive-
leaves; when the terraced hillside seemed to be powdering away;
when no sound reached the garden but the cry of a carter in the
road, the cooing of doves, stepping high along the eaves of the
gardener's shed, and the sound of the waterfall with its mysterious
retardations, a sound of bronze. I ate luncheon alone under a grape
arbor. The rest of the day was spent in roaming over the hills or
among the high chairs of Astrée-Luce's rich and curious library.

From the middle of the afternoon one sensed the approach of
dinner. One felt the gradual tightening of the chord of formality
until, like the bursting of some pyrotechnical bomb, full of
dazzling lights and fascinating detail, the ceremony began. For
hours there had come a hum as of bees from the wing of the house
that contained the kitchen; there followed the flights of maids and
hairdressers through the corridors, the candle-lighter, the flower-
bearers. The crushing of gravel under the window announces the
arrival of the first guests. The majordomo clasps on his golden
chain and takes his place with the footmen at the door. Mlle. de
Morfontaine descends from her tower kicking her train about to
teach it its flexibility. A string quartet on the balcony begins a waltz
by Glazounov as subdued as a surreptitious rehearsal. The evening
takes on the air of a pageant by Reinhardt. One passes to the
saloon. At the head of the table behind peaks of fruits and ferns,

or cascades of crystal and flowers, sits the hostess, generally in yellow satin, her high ugly face lit with its half-mad surprise. She generally supports a headdress of branching feathers and looks like nothing so much as a bird of the Andes blown to that bleakness by the coldest Pacific breezes.

I have described how Miss Grier brooded over her table and placed herself to hear every word whispered by her remotest guest. Astrée-Luce followed a contrary procedure and heard so little of what was said that her very guest of honor was often obliged to resign all hope of engaging her attention. She would seem to have been caught up into a trance; her eyes would be fixed on some corner of the ceiling as though she were trying to catch the distant slamming of a door. Generally some Cabalist held the opposite end of the table: Mme. Bernstein, huddled up in her rich fur cape, looking like an ailing chimpanzee and turning from side to side the encouraging amiability of her grimace; or the Duchess d'Aquilanera, a portrait by Moroni, her dress a little spotty, her face a little smudged, but somehow evoking all the passionate dishonest splendid barons of her line; or Alix d'Espoli making passes with her exquisite hands and transforming the guests into witty and lovable and enthusiastic souls. Miss Grier seldom came, having festivals of her own to direct. Nor was it often possible to invite the Cardinal, since any company to meet him must be chosen with infinite discretion.

Almost every evening after the last guest had left the hill or retired to bed, and the last servant had finished finding little things to adjust, Astrée-Luce and I would descend into the library and have long talks over a drop of *fine*. It was then that I began to understand the woman and to see where my first judgments had been wrong. This was not a silly spinster of vast wealth nourishing a Royalist chimaera; nor the sentimental half-wit of the philanthropic committees; but a Second-Century Christian. A shy religious girl so little attached to the things about her that she might awake any day and discover that she had forgotten her name and address.

Astrée-Luce has always illustrated for me the futility of goodness without intelligence. The dear creature lived in a mist of real piety; her mind never drifted long from the contemplation of her creator; her every impulse was goodness itself: but she had no brains. Her charities were immense but undigested; she was the prey of anyone who wrote her a letter. Fortunately her donations were small, for she lacked the awareness to be either avaricious or prodigal. I think she would have been very happy as a servant; she would have understood the role, have seen beauty in it, and if her position had been full of humiliation and trials it would have deeply nourished her. Sainthood is impossible without obstacles and she never could find any. She had heard over and over again of the sins of pride and doubt and anger, but never having felt even the faintest twinge she had passed through the earlier stages of the spiritual life in utter bewilderment. She felt sure that she was a wicked sinful woman, but did not know how to go about her own reform. Sloth? She had been on her knees an hour every morning before her maid appeared. So difficult, so difficult is the process of making oneself good. Pride? At last after intense self-examination she thought she had isolated in herself some vestiges of pride. She attacked them with fury. She forced herself to do appalling things in public in order to uproot the propensity. Pride of appearance or of wealth? She soiled her sleeves and bodice intentionally and suffered the silent consternation of her friends.

She read the lessons so literally that I have seen her give away her coat time after time. I have seen her walk miles with a friend who asked her to go as far as the road. Now I was to learn that her

fits of abstraction were withdrawals into herself for prayer and
adoration, and often caused by almost ludicrous incidents. I was no
longer left to wonder why all references to fish and fishing sent
her off into the clouds; I realized that the Greek word for fish was
the monogram of her Lord and acted upon her much as a
muezzin's call acts upon a Mohammedan. A traveller spoke flip-
pantly of the pelican; at once Mlle. de Morfontaine repaired to her
mental altar and besought its guest not to grieve at the disrespect
paid to one of His most vivid symbols. Strangest illustration of all
was shown me a little later. One day she chanced to notice on my
hall table an envelope which I had addressed to Miss Irene H.
Spencer, a teacher of Latin in the High Schools at Grand Rapids,
who had come over to put her hand on the Forum. At once Astrée-
Luce insisted on meeting her. I never told Miss Spencer why she
had been tendered so amazing a luncheon, why her hostess had
listened so breathlessly to her trivial travelogues, nor why on the
following day a golden chain hung with sapphires had been left at
the pension for her. In fact Miss Spencer was a devout Methodist
and would have been shocked to learn that IHS meant anything.

Strange though Mlle. de Morfontaine was, she was never ridiculous. Such utter refusal of self can by sheer excess become a substi-
tute for intelligence. Certainly she was able to let fall remarkably
penetrating judgments, judgments that proceeded from the intuition without passing through the confused corridors of our reason.
Though she was exasperating at times, at others she would abound
in almost miraculous perceptions of one's needs. People as diverse
as Donna Leda and myself had to love her, one moment almost
with condescension as to an unreasonable child, and the next with
awe, with fear in the presence of something of infinite possibility.
Whom were we entertaining unawares? Might this, oh literally! be
an . . . ?

This then was the being whom I came to know during those late conversations in the library over a drop of *fine*. The talk was leisurely, full of pauses and to no point, but my bruised instinct could no longer escape the conviction that there was some deeply important matter that she wished to submit to me. I soon foresaw that I was not to rest. My dread of the revelation however was heightened by the obvious difficulty Astrée-Luce found in coming to the point. Finally instead of trying to avoid the discussion I tried to provoke it; I thought I could help here and there by opening veins of conversation that might surprise her problem. But no. The happy moment hung off.

One evening, she asked me abruptly whether it would greatly interfere with my work if we were to move to Anzio for a few days. I replied that I should like nothing better. All I knew of Anzio was that it was one of the resorts on the sea, a few hours from Rome, the site of one of Cicero's villas, and near Nettuno. She added a little anxiously that we should have to go to a hotel, a very poor hotel at that, but that it was out of season and there were ways in which she could supply some of the deficiencies of the service. A little foresight could prevent my being too uncomfortable.

So one morning we climbed into the large plain car she reserved for travelling and drove westward. The back seat served as a warehouse. One glimpsed a maid, a prie-dieu, a cat, a real panel by Fra Angelico, a box of wines, fifty books and some window curtains. I found out later that there had been a lavish assortment of caviare, pâté, truffles and ingredients for rare sauces by which, with a discouraging failure to understand me, she intended to supplement the resources of a tourists' hotel. She drove, herself, and in nothing did Heaven's interest in her reveal itself more clearly. First we stopped at Ostia so that I might see the veritable spot where the last scene of my wretched play took place. We read aloud the page of Augustine and I silently vowed to renounce forever any notion of rephrasing it.

On our first evening at Anzio a cold wind blew in from the sea. The vines and shrubs whipped the houses; the lamps of the cafés about the square swung cheerlessly over wet tables; one could not escape the desolate slip-slap of the waves against the sea-wall. But we both had a taste for such weather. We decided at about six o'clock to walk to Nettuno returning for dinner at half-past nine. We wrapped ourselves in rubber and started off, leaning against the wind and spray and feeling strangely exhilarated. For a time we walked in silence, but entering at last that portion of the road that lies between the high walls of the villas, Astrée-Luce began to talk:

I have told you before, Samuele (the whole Cabala had followed the Princess in calling me Samuele), that the hope of my life is to see a king reigning in France. How impossible such a thing seems now! No one knows it better than I. But everything I love most is improbable. And it is the fact that it seems so untimely that will help us most when we come to prepare the Divine Right of Kings as a dogma of the Church. What anger there will be, what sneers! Even important Churchmen will rush down to Rome and beg us not to upset the progress of Catholicism by such a move. There will be controversies. All the newspapers and the reviews will be shouting and weeping and laughing and the whole basis of democratic government, the folly of republics, will be aired. Europe will be cleansed of the poison in its side. We have nothing to fear from debates. The people will turn to God and ask to be ruled by those houses of His choosing.—However, I am not trying to convince you of it now, Samuele; I am only stating it so as to lead up to something else. You are a Protestant; does this make you impatient? Are you tired of me?

No, no, please. I am very interested, I replied.

At that moment our road brought us again to the water's edge. We stood for a moment on a parapet looking down on the loud sea that plunged about on the washing stones of a village. It began to rain. Astrée-Luce was gripping the iron railing watching the steam that rose from the waves; she was crying silently.

Perhaps, she continued, as we returned to our journey, you can imagine the tenth part of my disappointment as I watch the Cardinal getting older, and myself, and the nations falling deeper and deeper into error, and so little done. He can help us. He seems to me to have been especially created to help us. I do not forget his work in China. It was heroic. But what a greater work remains for him in Europe. Year follows year and still he sits up there on the Janiculum, reading and walking in the garden. Europe is dying. He will not stir.

At the time I was deeply moved. The rain and her tears and the puddles and the slapping noises of the water against the seawall had begun to affect me. All the voices of nature kept repeating: Europe is Dying. I would have liked to stop and have a good meaningless cry myself, but I had to listen to the voice beside me:

I cannot understand why he does not write. Perhaps I am not meant to understand. I know he believes that the universality of the Church is imminent. I know that he believes that a Catholic Crown is the only possible rule. But he does not stir to help us. All we ask from him is a book on the Church and the States. Think, Samuele, his learning, his logic, his style—but you have never heard him preach? His irony in controversy and his amazing perorations! What would be left of Bosanquet? The constitutions of the republics of the world would be tossed about—you will forgive me if I seem disrespectful to your great country—tossed about like eggshells. His book would not be just a book fallen from the press: it would be a force of nature; it would be the simultaneous birth of an idea in a thousand minds. It would be placed at once in the canon and bound up with the Bible. And yet he spends his day among rose bushes and rabbits and reading histories of this and that. I want to do this in my lifetime; I want to arouse this great man to his task. And you can help me.

I was excited. The air was full of a divine absurdity. Here was someone who was not afraid of using superlatives. This was being mad on a great scale. It would be hard to come down to ordinary living after these intoxicating threats against the presidents of this world and the binderies of the British Bible Society. I tried to think of something to say. I mumbled something about willingness.

She did not notice my inadequacy. It seems to me, she continued, that I have at last discovered one of the causes of his reluctance to join us. But first, tell me how he is regarded by the various Romans whom you have met. What is his legend among people who do not know him?

Here I was frightened. Could *she* have heard? How could any of those strange rumors have reached her?

But she would learn nothing from me. I took leave of good faith and told her all the favorable reports I had heard. Simple souls were captivated by the thought that apart from a few major obligations he lived on sixty-five lire a week; that he spoke twelve languages; that he enjoyed polenta; that he visited in certain Roman homes (her own, in particular) without ceremony; that he was translating the Confessions and the Imitation into exquisite Chinese. I knew Romans who so loved the very thought of him that they took walks to the Janiculan Hill solely to peer between his garden gates and lurked about the house in the hope of giving their children an opportunity to kiss his ring.

Astrée-Luce waited in silence. At last she said with only a trace
of reproach:

You are trying to spare me, Samuele. But I know. There are
other stories about him. His enemies have been at work systemati-
cally poisoning his prestige. We know that there is no one in
Rome who is kinder, more humble, higher-minded; but among the
common people he has almost the reputation of a monster. Some
people have been at work spreading such rumors deliberately. And
the Cardinal has heard of them: through the whispering of
servants or by cries in the road, or by anonymous letters, in all sorts
of ways. He exaggerates this attitude. He feels that he is in a
hostile world. It has made his old age tragic. And that is why he
will not write. Yet it is within our power to save him still.—But
look! There is a francobollo shop. Let us get some cigarettes and
find some place to sit down. It makes me so happy to talk of
this!

Provided with cigarettes we looked about for a wine shop. Our
wish evoked one at the next curve in the road, a smoky uncordial
tunnel, but we sat down before the glasses of sour inky wine and
continued our conspiracy. Astrée-Luce confessed that if the ill-odor
had become attached to the Cardinal's name through any real
delinquencies on his part, we could not have hoped to dissipate it.
Truth in such subtle regions as rumor would be unalterable. But
she knew that the aspersions in this case were the result of a clever
campaign and she felt sure that a countercampaign could still
sweeten his reputation. In the first place our enemies had taken
advantage of the Italians' prejudice against the Orient. An Italian
enjoys the same delicious shudder at the sight of a Chinaman that
an American boy does at the mention of a trapdoor over a river.
The Cardinal had returned from the East yellow, unwrinkled. His
walk troubled them. It was easy to build upon this, to pass the

whisper along the Trasteverine underworld that he kept strange images, that animals (his gardenful of rabbits and ducks and guinea fowl) could be heard shrieking late at night, that his faithful Chinese servant had been seen in all sorts of terrifying attitudes. Next, his frugal life stirred their imaginations. Every one knew he was fabulously wealthy. Rubies as big as your fist and sapphires like doorknobs, where were they? Did you ever go up to the gate of the Villino Wei Ho? Come with me Sunday. If you sniff hard enough you can get the strangest odor, one that will leave you drowsy for days and give you dreams.

We were to change all this. We sat there choosing a committee of rehabilitation. We were to have magazine articles, newspaper paragraphs. His eightieth birthday was approaching. There would be presentations. Mlle. de Morfontaine was donating a Raphael altar piece to his titular church. But most of all we would send out agents among the people, telling them of his goodness, his simplicity, his donations to their hospitals, and ever so faintly his sympathy with socialistic ideas; he was to be the People's Cardinal. We had anecdotes of his snubbing the arrogant members of the College, of his defending a poor man who had stolen a chalice from his church. China was to be re-created for the Trasteverines. And so on. We were to prop up the Cardinal so that the Cardinal could prop up Europe.

When we returned to the hotel that night Astrée-Luce seemed to have grown ten years younger. Apparently I was the first person to whom she had outlined her vision. She was so eager to be at work that she suddenly asked me if I minded packing up again and going back to Tivoli that night. We could the better start work in the morning. What she really wanted was the exhilaration and fatigue of driving (her terrible driving) before she went to bed. So we put back into the car the maid, the Fra Angelico, the ingredients for sauces and the cat, and returned to the Villa Horace at about two in the morning.

The Cardinal was not to know that we were putting up a scaffolding about his good name and freshening the colors; but we were to persuade him not to do some of the things that particularly antagonized the public. The very next morning Astrée-Luce shyly begged me to go and see him. She did not know why, but she had a vague idea that now I knew her hopes my eyes would be open to significant details.

I found him as one could find him every sunny day the year round, seated in the garden, a book on his knee, a reading glass in his left hand, a pen in his right, a head of cabbage and a Belgian hare at his feet. A pile of volumes lay on the table beside him: *Appearance and Reality,* Spengler, *The Golden Bough, Ulysses,* Proust, Freud. Already their margins had begun to exhibit the spidery notations in green ink that indicated a closeness of attention that would embarrass all but the greatest authors.

He laid aside his magnifying glass as I came up the path of shells. *Eccolo, questo figliolo di Vitman, di Poe, di Vilson, di Guglielmo James,—di Emerson, che dico!* What do you want?

Mlle. de Morfontaine wants you to come to dinner Friday night, just the three of us.

Very good. Very nice. What else?

What do you want, Father, for your birthday? Mlle. de Morfontaine wants me to sound you tactfully . . .

Tactfully!—Samuelino, walk to the back of the house and tell my sister you will stay to lunch. I am to have a little Chinese vegetable dish. Will you have that or a little risotto and chestnut-paste? You can buy yourself something solid on the way down hill. How is Astrée-Luce?

Very well.

A little illness would be good for her. I am uncomfortable when

I am with her. There are certain doctors, Samuele, who are not happy when they are talking to people in good health. They are so used to the supplicating eyes of patients that say: Shall I live? In the same way I am ill at ease in the company of persons who have never suffered. Astrée-Luce has eyes of blue porcelain. She has a fair pure heart. It is sweet to be in the company of a fair pure heart, but what can one say to it?

There was St. Francis, Father . . . ?

But he had been libertine in his youth, or thought he had.— Senta! Who can understand religion unless he has sinned? who can understand literature unless he has suffered? who can understand love unless he has loved without response? *Ecc!* The first sign of Astrée-Luce's being in trouble was last month. There is a certain Monsignore who wants her millions for his churches in Bavaria. Every few days he climbs the hill to Tivoli and breathes into her ear: *And the rich He hath sent empty away.* The poor child trembles and pretty soon Bavaria will have some enormous churches, too ugly for words. Oh, you know, there is for every human being one text in the Bible that can shake him, just as every building has a musical note that can overthrow it. I will not tell you mine, but do you want to know Leda d'Aquilanera's? She is a great hater, and they say that during the Pater Noster she closes her teeth tight upon: *Sicut et nos dimittimus debitoribus nostris.*

At this he laughed for a long time, his body shaking in silence.

But was not Astrée-Luce devoted to her mother? I asked.

No, she has had no losses. That was when she was ten. She has poetized her, that is all.

Father, why did not that literal faith of hers carry her to a convent?

She promised her dying mother she would stay alive to put a Bourbon on the throne of France.

How can you laugh, Father, at her devotion to . . .

We old men are allowed to laugh at things that you little students may not even smile about. Oh, oh, the house of Bourbon. Would you be surprised if I gave up my life to reviving the royal brother-and-sister marriages of Egypt? Well! It is not more impossible.

Dear Father, won't you write one more book? Look, you have about you all the greatest books of the first quarter of my century . . .

And very stupid they are, too.

Won't you make us one. Such a great book, Father Vaini. About yourself, essays like Montaigne,—about China and about your animals and Augustine . . .

Stop! No! Stop at once. You frighten me. Do not you see that the first sign of childhood in me will be the crazy notion that I should write a book? Yes, I could write a book better than this ordure that your age has offered us (and with a sharp blow he pushed over the tower of books; the Belgian hare gave a squeal as he barely escaped being pinned under Schweitzer's *Skizze*). But a Montaigne, a Machiavelli . . . a . . . a . . . Swift, I will never be. How horrible, how horrible it would be if you should come here some day and find me writing. God preserve me from the last folly. Oh, Samuele, Samuelino, how bad of you to come here this morning, and awaken all the vulgar prides in an old peasant. No, don't pick them up. Let the animals soil them. What is the matter with this Twentieth Century of yours . . . ? You want me to compliment you because you have broken the atom and bent light? Well, I do, I do.—You may tell our rich friends, tactfully, that I want for my birthday a small Chinese rug now reposing in the window of a shop on the Corso. It would be unbecoming for me to say more than that it is on the left as you approach the Popolo.—The floor of my bedroom is getting colder

every morning, and I always promised myself that when I became
eighty I might have a rug in my bedroom.

What went wrong?

The first hour was delightful. The Cardinal always ate very
little (never meat) and that with preposterous slowness. If his
soup took him ten minutes his rice required half an hour. To be
sure the elements of trouble were present merely in these friends'
characters. They were so different that just to hear them talking
together had an air of high comedy. First, Astrée-Luce made the
mistake of referring to the Bavarian Monsignore. She suspected
that the Cardinal was out of sympathy with any plans she might
have of helping the Church in that direction; she longed to talk
over with him the problem of her wealth and its disposition, but
he refused to give her the least advice. He had endless resources of
ingenuity in evading the subject. As Rome was arranged at that
time it was most important that he should exercise no influence on
that aspect of his friend's life. Yet he allowed it to be seen that he
knew she would handle the matter foolishly. It ailed him to see
such an enormous instrument for progress drift down the wind of
ecclesiastical administration.

Now we must remember that it was the eve of his eightieth
birthday. We have already seen that the event had precipitated a
flood of amused bitterness. As he said later, he should have died at
the moment of leaving his work in China. The eight years that had
elapsed since then had been a dream of increasing confusion.
Living is fighting and away from the field the most frightening
changes were taking place in his mind. Faith is fighting, and now
that he was no longer fighting he couldn't find his faith anywhere.
This vast reading was doing something to him. . . . But most of
all we must remember his terror at the thought that the people of

Rome hated him. He would leave in dying a memory without affection and without dignity. An anonymous letter had told him that even in Naples children were kept in good behavior with threats that the Yellow Cardinal would skin them. If one were young one would laugh at such a rumor, but being old one grew cold. He was leaving a world where he was shuddered at for a world that was no longer as distinct as it had been, but which might yet have this consolation that he would not be able to look down from it and see the people surreptitiously spitting on the endings in *issimus* that would compose his epitaph.

Before I knew it we were in the middle of a wrangle about prayer. Astrée-Luce had always longed to hear the Cardinal discourse upon abstract matters. She had often tried to draw him into arguments on the frequent communion and on the invocation of the saints. He had once whispered to me that she was trying to extract from him the materials for a calendar, such sweet manuals as she could buy in the Place Saint Sulpice. Every word of his was sacred. She would not have hesitated to put him in a Church window with St. Paul. It was only after a few moments that she became aware that he was saying some rather strange things. Could that be Doctrine? If anything he said was difficult all she had to do was to try hard to grasp it. Truth, new truth. So she listened, first with surprise, then with mounting terror.

He was launched upon the paradox that in prayer one should never ask for anything. His dialectic was doing an incredible work. He had decided to be Socratic and was asking Astrée-Luce questions. He wrecked her on several orthodox assumptions. Twice she fell into heresy and was condemned by the councils. She seized hold of St. Paul but the epistle broke in her hand. She came to the surface for the third time but was struck by a Thomist fragment.

The previous week the Cardinal had been called to the deathbed of a certain Donna Matilda della Vigna, and it was poor Donna Matilda who was now dragged forth to point the argument. Exactly what had the survivors been praying for? Astrée-Luce was easily routed from the more obvious positions. She became frightened. Presently she rose:

I don't understand. I don't understand. You are joking, Father. Aren't you ashamed of saying such things to bewilder me, when you know how I value everything you say.

Look, then, continued the Cardinal. I shall ask Samuele about this. As he is only a Protestant it will be very easy to entangle him. Samuele, may I assume that God may have intended Donna Matilda to die before long anyway?

Yes, Father, for she died that very night.

But we thought that if we prayed very sincerely we might change His mind.

Why . . . there is authority for our hoping that in extremities our prayer may. . . .

But she died. Then we were not sincere enough! Or persevering enough! Good! Sometimes He grants and sometimes He doesn't, and Christians are expected to pray hard on the chance that this is one of the times He might relent. What a notion! Astrée-Luce, what a thought!

Father, I can't stay and hear you talk this way . . .

What a view of these things. Listen. It is incredible that He should change His mind. Because we frightened mortals are on the carpet? Oh! You are a slave to the idea of bargain. The money changers are still in the temple!

Here Astrée-Luce, gone quite white, returned to the arena with one more brave venture: But, Father, you know He answers the requests of a good Catholic. Then she added in a lower voice with tears in her eyes. But you were there, dear Father. If you had deeply wished it you could have altered the . . .

Here he half rose from his chair crying with terrible eyes: Insane child! What are you saying? I? *Have I no losses?*

Now she flung herself upon the floor before him. You have been saying these things to prove me. What is the answer? I will not let you go until you tell me. Dear Father, you know that prayer is answered. But your clever questions have upset all my old . . . old . . . What is the answer?

Come, sit down, my daughter, and tell me yourself. Think!

This went on for another half-hour. I grew more and more astonished. Mere prayer as a problem was soon left far behind. It was the idea of a benignant power behind the world that was being questioned now. For the Cardinal it was an exercise in rhetoric, sharpened by his temperamental scepticism on the one hand and by his latent resentment against Astrée-Luce on the other. It was a kind of questioning that would have had no effect on sound intellectual believers. It was disastrous for Astrée-Luce because she was a woman without a reason who just this once was trying to reason. She would so have liked to have been a deep thinker, and when she fell it was through her desire to be a different person.

It went on and on. At every fresh proposal he would now cry Bargain! A Bargain! and point out that her prayers sprang from fear or the greed for comfort. Astrée-Luce was going to pieces. I moved over behind her chair and pleaded with the Cardinal by gesture. Was he tormenting her out of caprice? Did he realize her devotion to himself?

At last she seemed to have a light:

My head is in a whirl. But I know now what you mean me to

answer. We may not ask for things, or people, or relief from sickness, but we may ask for spiritual qualities; for instance for the advancement of the Church . . . ?

Vanity! Vanity! How many years have we been praying for a certain good thing? What have statistics shown us?—I refer to the conversion of France.

With a cry Astrée-Luce rose and left the room. I took upon myself to protest to him.

She is foolish, Samuelino. You cannot call those convictions deep that were overturned with straws. No, trust me. This is for her good. I have been a confessor too long to go astray here. She has the spiritual notions of a school-girl. She must be fed on some harsher bread. Understand that she has never suffered. She is good. She is devout. But as I told you the other day, just by accident she has never known trouble.

Just the same, Eminence, I know her well enough to know that this very moment she is in her chapel, clinging to the altar-rails. She will be depressed for weeks.

But just at that moment Astrée-Luce returned. Her manner was agitated and artificially gracious. Will you excuse me if I go to bed now? she asked. (She never called him Father again.) Please stay and talk with Samuele.

No, no. I must be going. But before I go let me tell you one thing. The real truths are difficult. At first they are forbidding. But they are worth all the others.

I shall be thinking over what we have said.—I . . . I . . . Excuse me, if I ask you something?

Yes, my child, what is it?

Promise me you weren't joking.

I wasn't joking at all.

Did I really hear you say that the prayers of good men are of no . . . ? However. Goodnight. You will forgive my slipping away now?

So they took their leaves.

I went to bed worried. I was worrying about Astrée-Luce. Was she going to lose her faith? What do bystanders do in such a case? The loss of one's faith is always comic to outsiders, especially when the loser is in fine health, wealth, and a fairly sound mind. The loss of any one or all of these has a sort of grandeur; Astrée-Luce should have the loss of her faith depend on one of the others. It's not a thing one loses in fine weather.

I was wakened from a troubled sleep by a discreet but continuous knocking upon my door. It was Alviero, the majordomo.

Madame says will you please dress and come to her in the library, please.

What's the matter, Alviero?

I do not know, Signorino. Madame have not slept all night. She have been in the church hitting the floor.

All right, Alviero, I'll be there in a minute. What time is it?

Three o'clock and one-half, Signorino.

I dressed rapidly and hurried to the library. Astrée-Luce was still in her gown. Her face was white and drawn; her hair was disheveled. She came toward me with both hands extended: You will forgive my sending for you, won't you? I want you to help me. Tell me: were you made unhappy by the strange things Cardinal Vaini said after dinner?

Yes.

Have you Protestants ideas on these things?

Oh, yes, Mlle. de Morfontaine.

Were his ideas new? Is that what everyone is thinking?

No.

Oh, Samuele, what has happened to me! I have sinned. I have sinned the sin of doubt. Shall I ever have peace again? Can the

Lord take me back after I have had such thoughts? Of course, of course, I believe that my prayers are answered, but I have lost . . . the . . . the reason why I believe it. Surely, there is a key here. Perhaps it's just one word. All you have to do is find the one little argument that makes the whole thing natural. Isn't it strange! I've been looking here (and she pointed at the table which was covered with open books, the Bible, Pascal, the Imitation) but I don't seem to be able to put my finger on the right place. Sit down and try and tell me, my dear friend, what arguments there are that God hears us speak and will answer us.

I talked to her for quite a long while, but achieved nothing. Perhaps I even made it worse. I told her that I was sure that she still believed. I showed her that the very fact that she was distressed about it proved that she was furiously believing. After an hour of this wrestling she seemed a little comforted, however, and picking up a fur coat went back to her cold chapel and prayed diligently for faith until the morning.

At about ten she appeared in the garden and asked me to read a note that she was sending to the Cardinal. I was to pass on it. Dear Cardinal Vaini, I will always honor you above all my friends. I think you love me and wish me well. But in your great learning and multiple interests you have forgotten that we who are not brilliant must cling to our childhood beliefs as best we may. I have been inexpressibly troubled since yesterday evening. I want to ask a favor of you: that you indulge my weakness to the extent of not touching upon matters of belief when I am with you. It gives me great pain to have to ask you this. I beg of you to understand it as apart from any personal feelings of unfriendliness. I hope that I may grow strong enough to talk of these matters with you again.

It was a very bad letter, but that was perhaps due to the content. I suggested shyly that she omit the last sentence. So she copied it and sent it off by a special messenger.

Soon the day came for the end of my stay in the Villa. She came up to my room for a last talk.

Samuele, you have been with me during the saddest days of my life. I cannot deny that all interest has gone out of living for me. I still believe, but I don't believe as I used to. Perhaps it was not right that I went through life as I did. Now I know that I rose up every morning full of unspeakable happiness. It seldom left me. I had never thought before that my beliefs in themselves were unbelievable. I used to boast that they were, but I did not know what I was saying. Now hours come to me when I hear a voice saying: There is no prayer. There is no God. There are people and trees, millions of them both, every moment dying.—You will come and see me again, won't you, Samuele? Have I made it very unpleasant for you in the house?

When I reached my rooms in Rome I found three letters from the Cardinal asking me to come and see him at once. As I entered the gate he came toward me eagerly:

How is she? Is she well?

No, Father, she is in great trouble.

Come inside, my son. I must speak to you.

When we entered his study, he closed his door behind him, and said with great emotion: I want to say to you that I have sinned, greatly sinned. I cannot rest until I have tried to repair the harm I have done. Look, look at this letter she has written me.

Yes, I have seen it.

Her letter forbids my explaining what I meant. Is there no way I can reassure her?

There is only one way now. You must regain all her confidence before you touch on such matters again. You must come and go about her house as though nothing had happened—

Oh, but she will never ask me again!

Yes, she is having you all to dinner quite soon, Alix, Donna Leda, and M. Bogard.

Thanks be to God! I thank Thee, I thank Thee, I thank Thee, I thank Thee . . .

May I speak quite boldly, Eminence?

Yes. I am a poor old man, all mistakes. Speak to me as you like.

If you go, take great care not to let slip any remark on religious matters. I beg of you, do *not* try to reinstate yourself with some orthodox comments. She might misunderstand one little word and think you were attacking her faith again. It is very serious. Your ideas are not orthodox, Father, and if you said an orthodox thing it would not sound sincere and that would be worst of all. But if you come and go simply and affectionately, she will lose her horror of you—

Horror of me!

Yes, and very gradually, perhaps after a year, you may be able—

But I may not live a year!

Es muss sein!

This struck him as humorous and ruefully he sang Beethoven's phrase, adding: All the avenues of life lead to that.

Es muss sein. I should have stayed in China. (Here he fell silent for a while, heaving deep sighs and staring at his yellow hands.) God has chosen to take away my reason. I am an idiot, falling into every ditch. Oh, that I had died long ago—and yet I cannot die until I have righted myself. Hand me that red book behind you. There are two plays about old men, Samuelino, that grow dearer every day to an old man. There is your Lear, and—and opening *Oedipus at Colonus* he translated slowly:

Generous son of Aegeus, to the gods alone old age and death come never. But all else is confounded by all-mastering time. The strength of earth decays and the strength of the body. Faith dies. Distrust is born. Among friends the same spirit does not last true . . . and bowing his head he let the book fall to the floor. *Es muss sein.*

I did not go to that dinner. I dined alone with Miss Grier in the city, but at about ten we drove out to Tivoli to sit with the company. As we went I outlined to her discreetly the relations that now existed between two of her best friends: Oh, how stupid he is, she cried. How cruel! What a lot he has forgotten. Don't you see that the whole thing rests, not on the abstract question as to whether her prayers may be answered, but on the question as to whether ONE prayer may be answered? Her prayer for France . . . Doesn't he believe such things are real to other people?

He thinks that a little doubt will be good for her. He describes her as the woman who has never suffered.

He is in his dotage. I am so angry I am ill.

At this moment our car drew aside to let pass another hurrying by towards Rome. This was Mlle. de Morfontaine's great ugly travelling car and the Cardinal was in it.

There he is now, cried Miss Grier. They must have broken up early.

Something's happened, I said.

Yes, something has very likely happened, God forgive us. If

everything were all right, Alix would be driving back with him. Our wonderful company is dissolving. Alix no longer trusts us. Leda is losing her good old commonsense. Astrée-Luce has quarrelled with the Cardinal. I'd better leave Rome and go back to Greenwich.

As we approached the Villa we became aware that something indeed must have happened. The front door was open. The servants were gathered in the hall whispering in front of the closed doors of the drawing rooms. As we entered these opened and Alix, Donna Leda and Mme. Bernstein appeared supporting a sobbing Astrée-Luce. They led her up the stairs to her tower. Miss Grier without questioning the servants as to what had happened, gently urged them to return to their rooms. We passed into the drawing room just in time to see M. Bogard leaving by another door and looking considerably shaken. We sat down in silence, our thoughts full of foreboding. Simultaneously we became aware of a faint odor of powder and smoke and glancing about my eye fell upon a rent near the ceiling beneath which a little pile of white dust had collected on the floor. Mme. Bernstein hurried in and after closing the door carefully behind her, came toward us:

Not a soul must hear of this. Oh, this must be kept so quiet. What a thing to happen! Anything is possible after this. What a blessing that no servants were in the room when . . .

Miss Grier asked her several times what had happened.

I know nothing. I can hardly believe my own senses, she cried. Astrée-Luce must have gone mad. Elizabeth, will you believe me when I tell you that we were sitting here quietly over our coffee— Look, look! I didn't see that hole in the ceiling before!—Isn't it all frightful?

Please, Anna, please tell us what happened!

I am.—There we were sitting over our coffee, talking in low

voices of this and that, when suddenly Astrée-Luce went over to the piano, picked up a revolver from among the flowers and shot at the good Cardinal.

Anna! is he hurt?

No. It didn't even come near him. But what a thing to happen! What on earth could have made her do such a thing! We were friends—we were all such good friends. I do not understand anything.

Try and think, Anna: did she say anything when she fired at him, or before she fired?

That's the strangest of all. You won't believe me. She called out: The Devil is here. The Devil has come into this room. At the Cardinal!

What had he been saying?

Nothing! Merely everyday things. We had been telling stories about the peasants. He had been telling us about some peasants he had come across on his walks outside S. Pancrazio.

Suddenly Alix appeared: Elizabeth, go to her quickly. She wants to see you. She is alone.

Miss Grier hurried out.

Alix turned to me:

Samuele, you know the majordomo better than we do. Will you go and tell him that Astrée-Luce has had a nervous breakdown. That she thought she saw a burglar at the window, and that she fired at him. It is so important for the dear Father's sake that no hint of this gets about.

I went out and found Alviero. He knew the explanation was insufficient, but utterly devoted to the whole Cabala he could be trusted to dress the story at exactly the points that would most convince the other servants.

Alix did not understand what lay back of the shot, but she was

able to recall the conversation that had led up to it. The Cardinal
had told the following simple story, an incident he had witnessed
in one of his walks outside the city wall:

A farmer wished to break his six-year-old daughter of crying.
One afternoon he led her by the hand to the center of a marshy
waste, thickly grown with wiry reeds well above the child's head.
There he had suddenly flung away her hand, saying: Now are you
going to cry any more? The child, with a last rush of contrary pride
and with a beginning of fear, started to cry. All right, shouted the
father, we don't want any bad children in our house. I'm going to
leave you here with the tigers. Goodbye. And jumping out of the
child's sight, repaired to a wine shop at the edge of the waste and
sat down for an hour's cardplaying. The child strayed about from
hummock to hummock, wailing. In due time the father reappeared
and taking her affectionately by the hand led her home.

That was all.

But Astrée-Luce had never learned, as the rest of us have, to
harden her heart slightly before stories of cruelty or injustice. She
may have had no losses of her own, but she had always been ready
to expose her imagination to the full force of other people's
wrongs. Such an anecdote would have drawn from others a sigh, a
swift protective contraction of the lips and a smile of gratitude for
its safe conclusion. But to Astrée-Luce it was the vividest reminder
that the God whose business it was to brood over the world minis-
tering to the discouraged and the mistreated, was no more. The
Cardinal had killed him. There was no one left to soothe the horse
that has been beaten to death. The kittens that the boys fling
against the wall have no one to speak for them. The dog in torment that keeps his eyes upon her face, and licks her hands even
while his eyes grow dim, shall have no comforter but her. This was
not a casual story the Cardinal was telling: it concealed a covert

allusion to their conversation of the preceding week. It was a taunt. It was a sort of curse. Look at the world without God, he was saying. Get used to it. If she had lost God, oh how clearly she had gained the Devil. Here he was triumphing in this lacerating story. Astrée-Luce went over to the piano, picked up a revolver from the flowers and shot at the Cardinal, crying: The Devil has come into this room!

As the Cardinal drove back that night he kept repeating to himself the words: Then these things are real! It had required Astrée-Luce's shot to show him that belief had long since become for him a delectable game. One piled syllogism on syllogism, but the foundations were diaphanous. He strained to remember what faith was like when he had had it. He kept dragging before his mind's eye the young priest in China exhorting the families of the Mandarins. That was himself. Oh, to retrace the way. He would go back to China. If he could look again on the faces that were serene with a serenity he had given them, perhaps he could steal it back. But side by side with this hope was a terrible knowledge: no words could describe the conviction with which he saw himself guilty of the greatest of all sins. Murder was child's play compared to what he had done.

The firing of the shot had done as much for Astrée-Luce. On awaking, her terror lest she had harmed him, later her fear that she had fallen out of reach of his forgiveness was greater than had been her misery in a world without faith. It was given to me to carry from each to the other the first messages of anxious affection. When Astrée-Luce and the Cardinal discovered that they were living in a world where such things could be forgiven, that no actions were too complicated but that love could understand, or dismiss them, on that day they began their lives all over again. This reconciliation was never put into words, in fact it remained to the end merely in a state of hope. They longed to see one another again, but it would have been impossible. They dreamed of one of those long conversations that one never has on earth, but which one projects so easily at midnight, alone and wise; words are not rich enough nor kisses sufficiently compelling to repair all our havoc.

He received permission to return to China, and sailed within a few weeks. Several days after leaving Aden he fell ill of a fever and knew that he was to die. He called the Captain and the ship's doctor to him and told them that if they buried him at sea they would have to face the indignation of the Church, but that they would be fulfilling his dearest wish. He took what measures he could to shift upon himself the blame for such an irregularity. Better, better to be tossing in the tides of the Bengal Sea and to be nosed by a passing shark, than to lie, a sinner of sinners, under a marble tomb with the inevitable *insignis pietate,* the inescapable *ornatissimus.*

BOOK FIVE

THE DUSK OF THE GODS

When my time came to leave Rome I set aside several days for the last offices of piety, piety in the Roman sense. I wrote a note to Elizabeth Grier arranging for a long late talk on the eve of my departure. There are some questions I want to ask you, I said, which no one can answer. Then I went to the Villino Wei Ho and sat for an hour with the Cardinal's sister. The guinea fowl were less vocal than formerly and the rabbits were still hobbling about the garden looking for a gleam of violet. I went to Tivoli and peered through the iron gates of the Villa Horace. Already it looked as though no one had lived there for years. Mlle. de Morfontaine had returned to her estates in France and was living in the closest retirement. They said that she opened no letters, but I wrote her a note of farewell. I even spent an afternoon in the stifling rooms of the Palazzo Aquilanera, where Donna Leda imparted to me in great confidence the news of her daughter's engagement. Apparently the young man was unable to produce any cousins from among the draughty courts of Europe; his family was merely Italian; but he owned a modern palace. At last a bathroom was to make its appearance in the house of Aquilanera. How time flies!

My most considerable observance was a trip to Marcantonio's grave. I found it by the village cemetery near the Villa Colonna-Stiavelli. Consecrated ground had been denied the boy, but in her bewilderment and love the mother had contrived a false wall of stones and briars that seemed to include his grave among those of souls that the Church felt safe in recommending at the Judgment Day. Here I sat down and prepared to think about him. I was perhaps the only person in the world who understood what had brought him there. The last office of friendship would be to think about him. But some birds were singing; a man and his wife were cultivating the ground in the next field; the sunlight was heavy. Hard as I tried I could not keep my thoughts on my friend; it was not difficult to recall his features or to meditate about dissipation; but really elegiac reflection escaped me, Marcantonio. I drove back to Rome ashamed of myself. But it had been a delightful day in the country, unforgettable June weather.

There was one association I could not renew; I could not go to see Alix. Whenever I met her by chance the barrier of her lowered eyelids told me that we would never have long talks again.

Closing the apartment was melancholy enough. Ottima and I spent hours in packing, our heads bent over our boxes and full of our imminent farewells. She was going back to her wine-shop at the corner. Long before I bought a ticket she had begun to pray for those in peril on the sea and to notice the windy days. After an exhausting struggle with myself I decided to give her the police dog. Kurt's affections were equally divided between us; in Europe or in America he would pine for an absent friend. Ottima and

Kurt would grow old together in a life filled with exquisite mutual attentions. I could swear that before I went to the hotel on that last night Kurt knew I was taking leave of him. There was a grandeur I fell short of in the way he faced an inevitable situation. He placed one paw on my knee and looked to the right and left in deep embarrassment. Then lying down he placed his muzzle between his paws and barked twice.

I found Elizabeth Grier at midnight sitting in the library that Blair had catalogued. Her small neat head looked tired and after some desultory conversation I made a move to go. She reminded me that I had intended asking her some questions.

My questions are harder to put than to answer.

Try.

Miss Grier, did you know that you and your friends were called the Cabala?

Yes, of course.

I shall never know such a company again. And yet there seems to be some last secret about you that I've never been able to seize. Haven't you anything to tell me that will show me what you all meant, how you found one another, and what made you so different from anyone else?

Miss Grier took a few minutes off to think this over. She sat smiling strangely and stroking with her fingertips the roots of her hair beside her left temple. Yes, she said, but it will only make you angry if I tell you. Besides it's very long.

It's not long, Miss Grier, but you will insist on making it long because you hate to have your guests leave before dawn. However, I shall listen to you for hours if you promise to throw some light on the Cabala and the dinners at the Villa Horace.

Well, first you must know, Samuele, that the gods of antiquity did not die with the arrival of Christianity.—What are you smiling at?

You're adorable. You have resolved to make your explanation last forever. I asked about the Cardinal and you have gone back to Jupiter. What became of the gods of antiquity?

Naturally when they began to lose worshipers they began to lose some of their divine attributes. They even found themselves able to die if they wanted to. But when one of them died his godhead was passed on to someone else; no sooner is Saturn dead than some man somewhere feels a new personality descending upon him like a strait-jacket, do you see?

Now, Miss Grier!

I told you it would make you angry.

You don't pretend this is true?

I won't tell you whether this is true, or an allegory, or just nonsense.—Next, I am going to read you a strange document that came into my hands. It was written by a certain Hollander who became the god Mercury in 1912. Will you listen?

Has it anything to do with the Cabala?

Yes. And with you. For I sometimes think that you are the new god Mercury. Take some of that claret and listen quietly.

I was born in a Dutch parsonage in 1885. I was the despair of my home and the terror of the village, a little liar and thief in the full enjoyment of my health and wit. My real life began one morning of my twenty-seventh year when I experienced the first of a series of violent pains in the center of my head. This was my deification. Some untender hand was emptying the cup of my skull of its silly gray brains and filling it with the divine gas of instinct. My body too had its part in this; each microscopic cell had to be transformed; I was not to fall sick or grow old or die, save when I chose. As historian of the gods I have to keep record of an accident whereby, through some monstrosity in spiritual law, an Apollo of the Seventeenth Century failed to completely deify: one arm remained corruptible.

It was then that I discovered the first great attribute of our nature, namely that to wish for a thing is to command it. It does not suddenly fall into your hand or descend in a rosy mist upon your carpet. But circumstances start a discreet ballet about you and the desired thing comes your way through the neatest possible imitation of natural law and probability. Scientists will tell you that they have never seen the sequence of cause and effect interrupted at the instance of prayer or of divine reward or retribution. Do they think, the fools, that their powers of observation are cleverer than the devices of a god? The poor laws of cause and effect are so often set aside that they may be said to be the merest approximations. I am not merely a god but a planet and I speak of things I know. So I stole my mother's savings from under her pillow and went to Paris.

But it is at Rome that we were last worshiped under our own names, and it is thither that we are irresistibly called. During the journey I gradually discovered further traits of my new being. I woke up mornings to discover that bits of information had been deposited in my mind overnight, the enviable knowledge for instance, that I had the power of "sinning" without remorse. I entered the Porta del Popolo one midnight in June, 1912. I ran the length of the Corso, leapt the fence that surrounds the Forum, and flung myself upon the ruins of my temple. All night in the fine rain I tore my clothes in joy and anguish, while up the valley came an interminable and ghostly procession singing my hymns and hiding me in a tower of incense. With the coming of dawn my worshipers vanished and wings no longer fluttered at my heels. I climbed out of the sunken ruins and went out into the misty streets in search of some coffee.

Godlike I never reflect; all my actions arrive of themselves. If I pause to think I fall into error. During the next year I made a great deal of money on the races at Parioli. I speculated in motion pictures and African wheat. I went into journalism and the misrepresentations I sowed will have deferred Europe's recovery from the War many scores of years. I love discord among gods and men. I have always been happy. I am the happiest of the gods.

I had been called to Rome to serve as the gods' messenger and secretary, but more than a year had passed before I recognized even one. The Church of Santa Maria sopra Minerva is built over an ancient temple to that goddess and there one day I found her. So impatient was I to discover the others that I disobeyed the laws of my nature and went hunting for them. I spent hours hanging about the station in search of newly arrived divinities. One night I strode the platform waiting for the Paris Express. I was trembling with premonition. I had donned a silk hat and its complements, a coral camellia, and a little blonde moustache. Plumed with blue smoke and uttering splendid cries the train rushed into the station. The travelers descended from their compartments into a sea of *fachini* and relatives. I bowed to a Scandinavian diplomat and a Wagnerian prima donna. They returned my greeting hesitantly; a glance into their eyes showed me that they were brilliant but not supernatural. There was no incipient Bacchus among the Oxford students on vacation; the Belgian nuns on pilgrimage discovered me no Vesta. I scanned faces for half an hour until the length of pavement was deserted and a long line of old women with pails

appeared. I stopped by the engine to ask a guard if another section
of the train was to follow. I turned to see a strange face looking at
me from the small window of the locomotive—mis-shapen, black
with coal-dust, gleaming with perspiration and content, and grinning from ear to ear, was Vulcan.

Here Miss Grier raised her head: There follow fifty pages
describing his encounters with the others. Have you anything to
say? Do you recognize anything?

But, Miss Grier, I've had no headaches! I don't receive what I
want!

No?

What am I to understand? You've made it twice as confused.
Explain some more.

He goes on to say that the gods were afraid of being laughed at
for what they had lost. Flight, for instance, and invisibility, and
omniscience and freedom from care. People would forget that they
still had a few enviable powers: their strange elation; their command over matter; their ability to live or die when they chose and
to live beyond good and evil. And so on.

What became of him?

Finally he decided to die, as they all do. All gods and heroes are
by nature the enemies of Christianity—a faith trailing its aspira-
tions and remorses and in whose presence every man is a failure.
Only a broken will can enter the Kingdom of Heaven. Finally
tired out with the cult of themselves they give in. They go over.
They renounce themselves.

I was astonished at the desolation in her voice. It held me back
from eagerly demanding of her the application to the Cabala of all
these principles. We went into the next room where her musicians
were waiting to offer us some English madrigals. The applications

still occur to me, especially when I am depressed. They give in. They go over.

On the night that my steamer left the bay of Naples I lay sleepless in my deck-chair until morning. Why was I not more reluctant at leaving Europe? How could I lie there repeating the Aeneid and longing for the shelf of Manhattan? It was Virgil's sea that we were crossing; the very stars were his: Arcturus and the showery Hyades, the two Bears and Orion in his harness of gold. All these passed before me in a cloudless sky and in the water, murmuring before a light wind, the sliding constellations were brokenly reflected.

Mercury is not only the messenger of the gods; he is the conductor of the dead as well. If in the least part his powers had fallen to me I should be able to invoke spirits. Perhaps Virgil could read my mood for me, and raising my two palms I said in a low voice (not loud enough to reach the open port-holes behind me):

Prince of poets, Virgil, one of your guests and the last of barbarians invokes you.

For an instant I thought I saw the shimmer of a robe and the reflection of the starlight on the shiny side of a laurel leaf. I pressed my advantage:

O anima cortese mantovana, greatest of all Romans, out of the eternity of that limbo to which the Florentine, perhaps wrongly, consigned you, grant me a crumb of time.

Now indeed the shade stood in mid-air just above the hand-rail. The stars were glittering and the water was glittering, and the great shade, picked out in sparks, was glittering furiously. But the image must become clearer. There was one title that might avail more with him than those of poet or Roman.

Oh, greatest spirit of the ancient world and prophet of the new, by that fortunate guess wherein you foretold the coming of Him who will admit you to His mountain, thou first Christian in Europe, speak to me!

Now indeed the gracious spirit became completely visible with pulsations of light, half silver and half gold, and spoke:

Be brief, importunate barbarian. Except for this last salutation wherein you have touched my only pride, I would not delay here. Detain me not from the absorbing games of my peers. Erasmus is in debate with Plato, and Augustine has descended from the hill and sits among us, though the air is gray. Be brief, I pray you, and give heed to your Latin.

At this I realized that I had no definite question to put to my guest. In order to mark time and prolong so uncommon an interview, I engaged him in conversation:

Was I then right, Master, in assuming that Dante was not completely in God's confidence?

Indignation infused a saffron stain into the noble figure in silvergold: Where, where is he, that soul of vinegar, that chose to assign the souls of the dead more harshly than God? Tell him that though a pagan I too shall see bliss. It is nothing that I must first pay the penalty of ten thousand years. Behold this moment I exhibit the sin of anger; where is *he* in pain for the sin of pride?

I was a little shocked to discover that neither genius nor death removed us beyond the temptation to asperity, but said: Master, have you met the poets of the English tongue that have come into your groves?

Let us be brief, my friend.—One came that had been formerly blind and did me much honor. He spoke a noble Latin. Those that stood by assured me that in his lines mine were not seldom reflected.

Milton was indeed your son. . . .

But before him came another, greater than he, a writer of pieces for a theatre. He was proud and troubled and strode among us unseeing. He made me no salutation. Vanity no longer exists among us, but it is sweet to exchange greetings among the poets.

He knew but little Latin, Master, and perhaps had never read your page. Moreover in life he was neither the enemy nor advocate of grace and being arrived in your region his whole mind may well have been consumed with anxiety as to his eternal residence. Is he among you still?

He sits apart, his hand over his eyes, and only raises his head when, in the long green evenings, Casella sings to us, or when on the wind there drifts from Purgatory the chorus that one Palestrina prepares.

Master, I have just spent a year in the city that was your whole life. Am I wrong to leave it?

Let us be brief. This world where Time is, troubles me. My heart has almost started beating again,—what horror! Know, importunate barbarian, that I spent my whole lifetime under a great delusion,—that Rome and the house of Augustus were eternal. Nothing is eternal save Heaven. Romes existed before Rome and when Rome will be a waste there will be Romes after her. Seek out some city that is young. The secret is to make a city, not to rest in it. When you have found one, drink in the illusion that she too is eternal. Nay, I have heard of your city. Its foundations have knocked upon our roof and the towers have cast a shadow across the sandals of the angels. Rome too was great. Oh, in the pride of your city, and when she too begins to produce great men, do not forget mine. When shall I erase from my heart this love of her? I cannot enter Zion until I have forgotten Rome.— Dismiss me now, my friend, I pray thee. These vain emotions have shaken me. . . . (Suddenly the poet became aware of the Mediterranean:) Oh, beautiful are these waters. Behold! For many years I have almost forgotten the world. Beautiful! Beautiful!—But no! what horror, what pain! Are you still alive? Alive? How can you endure it? All your thoughts are guesses, all your body is shaken with breath, all your senses are infirm, and your mind ever full of the fumes of one passion or another. Oh, what misery to be a man. Hurry and die!

Farewell, Virgil!

The shimmering ghost faded before the stars, and the engines beneath me pounded eagerly toward the new world and the last and greatest of all cities.

THE WOMAN OF ANDROS

*The first part of this novel is based upon
the* Andria, *a comedy of Terence who in turn based
his work upon two Greek plays, now lost to us,
by Menander.*

The earth sighed as it turned in its course; the shadow of night crept gradually along the Mediterranean, and Asia was left in darkness. The great cliff that was one day to be called Gibraltar held for a long time a gleam of red and orange, while across from it the mountains of Atlas showed deep blue pockets in their shining sides. The caves that surround the Neapolitan gulf fell into a profounder shade, each giving forth from the darkness its chiming or its booming sound. Triumph had passed from Greece and wisdom from Egypt, but with the coming on of night they seemed to regain their lost honors, and the land that was soon to be called Holy prepared in the dark its wonderful burden. The sea was large enough to hold a varied weather: a storm played about Sicily and its smoking mountains, but at the mouth of the Nile the water lay like a wet pavement. A fair tripping breeze ruffled the Aegean and all the islands of Greece felt a new freshness at the close of day.

The happiest, and one of the least famous of the islands, Brynos, welcomed the breeze. The evening was long. For a time, the sound of the waves, briskly slapping against the wall of the little harbor, was covered by the chattering of women, by the shouts of boys, and by the crying of lambs. As the first lights appeared, the women retired; as the air was filled with the clangor of the shop fronts being put into place, the boys' voices ceased; and finally only the murmur of the men in the wine-shops, playing at games with ivory counters, mingled with the sounds from the sea. A confused star-light, already apprehensive of the still unrisen moon, fell upon the tiers of small houses that covered the slope and upon the winding flights of stairs that served as streets between them.

The wine-shops stood about the roughly paved square at the water's edge and in one of them the five or six principal fathers of the island sat playing. By the time the moon had risen, two of these, Simo and Chremes, had outstayed their companions. Simo was the owner of two warehouses; he was a trader and had three ships that passed continually to and fro among the islands. The men had finished playing; the counters lay on the table between them and they sighed into their beards as they thought of the long walk through the ghostly olive trees to their homes. Simo was more tired than usual: whereas the law of moderation teaches us that the mind cannot be employed for more than three hours daily over merchandise and numerals without soilure, he had that day spent five hours in argument and traffic.

"Simo," said Chremes suddenly, with the air of a man bracing himself to an unpleasant and long deferred task, "your boy is twenty-five now—"

Simo groaned as he saw the subject arising that he was never able to look in the face.

"It's four years," continued Chremes, "since you first said that a young man mustn't be forced into marriage by his old people. And certainly no one has been trying to force Pamphilus. But what is he waiting for? He helps you in the warehouse; he exercises in the field; he dines at the Andrian's. How many years must that kind of life go on before you agree with me that he would be better off married to my daughter?"

"Chremes, he must come to me of his own accord. I will not be the first one to speak about it to the boy."

"First! It won't be speaking of it first, Simo. It has been understood between our families for years that he will marry Philumena. It's being spoken of all the time. The young people tease him about it from morning to night. He knows perfectly well that my daughter is ready to marry him. It's sheer laziness on his part. It's sheer unwillingness to take on the responsibilities of being a husband and a father and the foremost young householder on the island."

"He's a young man who knows what he means to do. I will not coerce him."

"Then it's settled that he doesn't want to marry my daughter. It's a humiliation for her to be waiting all these years for him to make up his mind, and her mother's been after me to close the matter for a long time. Perhaps I shouldn't say it, but you'll be throwing away a good thing through sheer hesitancy, both of you. Philumena is by far the healthiest and the prettiest girl on any of these islands. And she's clever at everything that is expected of a woman in the home. The uniting of our two families has advantages, Simo, that I don't have to point out to you. But this lapse of time has made it clear that your son is going to wait until his fancy has been caught by some other girl, I suppose. So be it! From this very night my wife is going to start looking about for some other young man."

"Chremes, Chremes, he's only twenty-five. Let him play about a little longer. Why must they become husbands and fathers so soon? He's good and he's happy. So is your daughter. Let them be awhile."

"Grandchildren!—that's what I want to see. There shouldn't be a long step between the generations. It's bad for customs and manners."

"You'll make a greater mistake by hurrying than by delaying."

"Well," Chremes continued, "there's another reason why I want the matter settled soon. And that is this: we don't like the visits that Pamphilus is paying to the Andrian woman. Naturally, Simo, it's hard for me to be severe about it, because my own son goes there too. But it's natural that a father should be more exacting in regard to his son-in-law than in regard to his son."

Simo looked more uncomfortable than ever and remained silent. Chremes went on:

"I don't think you like this resort to foreign women any more than I do. Our islands have always been famous for strict and good behavior. If the devil was in us as boys we could always follow some shepherdess up a dark road. But this Andrian has brought the whole air of Alexandria to town with her, perfumes and hot baths and late hours."

Simo stroked his cheeks a moment and then replied in a low grunting voice: "Well, if it isn't one thing, it's another, I suppose. I don't know anything about this Andrian. The women seem to talk of nothing else from morning to night, but one can't believe what they say."

Thus invited, Chremes launched into his exposition with considerable relish, examining Simo's face from time to time to see if the details were arousing in him the interest they held for himself. "Her name is Chrysis, and I don't know what she means by calling herself Andrian. The island of Andros was never famous for such airs and graces as she puts on. She's flitted from Corinth and Alexandria, you may be sure. She should have stayed in her cities instead of burying herself in our town and reciting poetry to our young men. Yes, yes, she recites poetry to them like the famous

ones. She has twelve or fifteen of them to dinner every seven or
eight days,—the unmarried ones, of course. They lie about on
couches and eat odd food and talk. Presently she rises and recites;
she can recite whole tragedies without the book. She is very strict
with the young men, apparently. She makes them pronounce all
the Attic accents; they eat in the Athenian mode, drinking toasts
and wearing garlands, and each in turn is elected King of the
Banquet. And at the close, hot towels are passed around for them
to wipe their hands on."

Simo did not concede to Chremes the pleasure of his close interest; his eyes were lowered and his face wore the same bored expression that it brought to all island gossip. Chremes decided to be
less expansive and added with easy indignation: "As for me,
Alexandria is Alexandria and Brynos is Brynos. A few more im-
ported notions and our island will be spoiled forever. It will
become a mass of poor undigested imitations. All the girls will be
wanting to read and write and declaim. What becomes of home
life, Simo, if women can read and write? You and I married the
finest girls of our time and we've been happy. We can at least
provide one more generation of good sense and good manners on
this island before the age arrives when all the women will have the
airs of dancers and all the men go about waiting on them."

Simo knew the answer to this, but he repressed it. Chremes,
more than any man on the island, was ruled by his wife. In fact
from her loom in the shadow, Chremes's wife tried to rule the
whole island, using her harassed husband as her legislative and
punitive arm. Simo asked:

"What happens after the banquet?"

"Each boy pays for his plate, and pays right smartly too, and
from time to time one or another is graciously permitted to stay
until morning. That's all I know."

"Is your son at all these dinners?"

"He was quarreling or something,—or perhaps he drank too much, I don't know. At all events, he was expelled for a time. Thrown right out into the street, he was, by the other guests. But he's made his peace with her again."

"Do you talk to him about this . . . this Chrysis?"

"Why, no. I pretend to know nothing about it."

"Is my son always there?"

"They say he's practically always there."

There was a long pause. The boy who attended in the wine-shop went out into the moonlight and started putting up the shutters. Presently he returned and whispered to Simo that an old woman was waiting outside to speak to him and that she had been waiting there for some time. This was unusual on Brynos, but Simo took pride in never betraying any surprise. He nodded slightly and continued staring before him.

"Are there any other women at the Andrian's?" he asked.

"I don't know. Some say there are and some say there aren't. But there's a houseful of some sort. In fact it's a kind of hospital for the old and the lame and the . . . all kind of old battered pensioners. The house is way up at the edge of the town . . ."

"I know where it is."

". . . and the people, whoever they are, never come into town. They never even go out on the road by day. Oh, you can be sure the townspeople talk of nothing else."

Chremes rose and put on his cloak. He saw that Simo was as far as ever from committing himself. "Well, that's how it stands," he said. "I hope that in another ten days you can give me a more definite answer. My wife is after me a good deal, Simo, and she says that I'm to tell you this, that unless Pamphilus stops those visits all idea of a marriage between himself and Philumena is

impossible. And that any such marriage must be definitely settled
pretty soon or you'll have to start finding some other girl one-tenth
as good."

For the first time Simo bestirred himself and said slowly: "You
and your wife will be throwing away a good thing too, Chremes.
It's precisely because Pamphilus is a great deal more than an ordinary island boy that I can't speak to him as I could to another son.
There are more sides to Pamphilus than you imagine."

"Yes, Simo, we know that he's a fine young man. But we also
know, if you will forgive me, that there's a strain in Pamphilus of
the . . . the undecided, the procrastinating. To do his best and to
take his place, Pamphilus must be urged on by someone, like
yourself, whom he admires. And he's not as interested in this
island and in what it stands for as he should be. Do you know the
young priest of Aesculapius and Apollo? Well, there is something
of the priest in Pamphilus. Such people aren't interested in putting
their foot forward. They haven't yet come to see what life is
about."

Chremes went out and plodded home along the rocky road.
Simo sat on a minute longer. What a bad ending to a bad day, he
thought. The two men had grown up on the island together. For
thirty years they had been its leading citizens. They knew one
another too well. In their conversation they had let play the faint
antagonism that always lay between them. This boasting about
their children,—how vulgar, how unhellene. How unphilosophic.
Yet that was true: there was something of the priest in Pamphilus.

Simo turned to the old woman who was hiding in the shadow by
the door. "You wanted to speak to me?" he asked roughly.

Between fright and suspense—for she had been waiting there
for the greater part of two hours—Mysis was barely able to find

her voice. "My mistress wishes to speak to you, sir,—Chrysis, the Andrian," and she pointed with both hands toward the water-front.

Simo grunted. Looking up he saw the beautiful woman leaning against the parapet at the water's edge fifteen paces away. Her head and body were wrapped in veils, and she waited calmly and impersonally in the moonlight as though two hours were but a moment in her serenity. Below her in the little protected harbor the boats knocked against one another in friendly fashion, but all else was still under the melancholy and peace of the moon. Simo approached her without deference and said: "Well?"

"I am—" she began.

"I know who you are."

She paused and began again. "I am in an extremity. I am driven to ask a service of you." Simo pushed his lips forward, raised his eyebrows, and lowered his eyes wearily. She continued in an even voice without anxiety or suppliance: "A friend of mine is very ill on the island of Andros from which I come. Twice I have sent this friend money by the hands of various sea-captains going between the islands. I know now that the captains are dishonest and that my money never reaches him. All that I ask is that you put your frank upon the package of money and it will reach him."

Simo did not like to see women carrying themselves, as this Andrian did, with dignity and independence. His antagonism was increased; he asked abruptly: "Who is this friend?"

"He was formerly a sea-captain," she replied, still without servility. "But now he is not only ill; he is insane. He is insane by reason of the hardships he endured in the war. I have put him in charge of some people, but they will only be kind to him as long as I send them money for it. Otherwise they will put him away on a small island nearby with the others. You know such islands . . .

where basins of food are left for them every few days . . . and where—"

"Well," said Simo harshly, "since your friend has lost the use of his reason and since he cannot realize the conditions under which he lives, it is best that you leave him upon the island with the others. Is that not so?"

Chrysis tightened her lips and looked far out over his head. "I have no answer for that," she replied. "It may be true for you, but it is not true for me. This man was once a very famous sea-captain. You may have known him. His name was Philocles. Now I think I am his only friend, unless you choose to help him also."

Simo did not acknowledge having known him, but the tone in his next words was less vindictive. "When would you like this money to go?"

"I . . . I have some money ready now, but I would prefer to send some in ten days."

"What is your name?"

"My name is Chrysis, daughter of Arches of Andros."

"Chrysis, I will do this for you, and I will even add to the sum. In return you will do a favor for me. You will refuse my son entrance into your house."

Chrysis moved slightly to one side and stretching her arm along the parapet looked down into the harbor. "Favors cease to be favors when there are conditions attached to them, Simo. Magnanimity does not bargain with its powers." These maxims were almost murmured; then she raised her head and said to him: "I cannot do that, unless I tell your son that it is because you have ordered it."

Simo's slightly cynical superiority over the rest of the world reposed on the fact that he had gone through life without ever having been surprised as unjust, untruthful, or ungenerous. Angry, but with himself, for having been caught at this disadvantage, he replied: "That is not necessary. It would be quite simple for your servant to tell him that you do not wish him to come into the house."

"I could not do that. There are several young men on the island to whom my door, for one reason or another, is closed. I cannot do that to Pamphilus without giving him a reason. If you understood the spirit of our group you would not wish me to do that; I think that there we are not lacking in respect for one another. I hardly know your son; I have scarcely exchanged twenty words with him; but I know that he is by far the first young man among my guests." Suddenly the image of Pamphilus rose up before her and she was filled with an excitement and joy in praising him, and for that very reason she subdued herself and added in a lower voice: "He is old enough to make decisions for himself. And if I do this, he must understand."

Simo was aware that some strange wise praise of his son hovered between them and his heart almost stopped beating for pleasure, but from his lips there rushed the brutal phrase he had prepared a moment before: "Then you must send your money to Andros some other way."

"Very well," she said.

They stood looking at one another. Simo suddenly realized that he lived among people of thin natures and that he was lonely; he was out of practice in conversing with sovereign personalities whose every speech arose from resources of judgment and inner poise. With his wife, with Chremes, with the islanders one could talk with half one's mind and still hold one's authority, but here in a few moments this woman had caught him twice at a disadvantage. Chrysis saw this and came to his aid; she broke the silence that was leaving him obstinate, angry, and small.

"It is perhaps his younger brother whose life can be arranged for him; your Pamphilus deserves to be better understood than that." And her tone implied: "You and he are of one measure and should stand on the same side."

Simo preferred talking about his sons to any other activity in the world, but his emotions were very mixed as he assembled an answer to this remark:

"Well, well . . . Andrian, I will frank your money for you. I have boats going to Andros every twelve days. One went off today."

"I thank you."

"Could I ask you . . . euh . . . not to mention this to Pamphilus?"

"I shall not."

"Well . . . well, goodnight."

"Goodnight."

Simo trudged home in an unaccustomed elation. It made him happy to hear Pamphilus praised and "probably this woman was an exceptional judge of persons." He had made a fool of himself, but in good hands one does not mind. "Life . . . life . . . ," he said to himself, hunting for a generalization that would describe its diversity, its power of casting up from time to time on the waves of tedious circumstance such starlike persons. The generalization did not arrive, but he walked on in a bright astonishment. How he would like to hear her read a play; he used to be interested in such things and when his journeys took him to an island that was large enough to have a theatre he never missed an opportunity to hear a good tragedy.

As he entered the courtyard of his farm he saw Pamphilus standing alone, looking at the moon.

"Good evening, Pamphilus," he said.

"Good evening, father."

Simo went to bed, deeply moved with pride, but for form's sake he repeated anxiously to himself: "I don't know what I'll do with him. I don't know what I'll do with him."

And Pamphilus stood looking at the moon and thinking about his father and mother. He was thinking about them in the light of a story that Chrysis had told. As the banquets drew to a close she liked to move the conversation away from local comment and to introduce some debate upon an abstract principle. (She cited often the saying of Plato that the true philosophers are the young men of their age. "Not," she would add, "because they do it very well; but because they rush upon ideas with their whole soul. Later one philosophizes for praise, or for apology, or because it is a complicated intellectual game.") Pamphilus remembered that on one evening the conversation had turned upon the wrong that poets do in pretending that life is heroic. And a boy from the other end of the island had said, half-mockingly and half-hopefully: "Well, you know, Chrysis . . . you know, life in a family is not in the same world as life in Euripides."

Chrysis sat a moment searching for her answer, then she lifted her hand and said: "Once upon a time—"

The table burst out laughing, but with an affectionate laugh of mock-repudiation, because they knew that she liked to cast her remarks into the form of fables and to begin them with this childish formula. Pamphilus heard again her beautiful voice saying:

"Once upon a time there was a hero who had done a great service to Zeus. When he came to die and was wandering in the gray marshes of Hell, he called to Zeus reminding him of that service and asking a service in return: he asked to return to earth for one day. Zeus was greatly troubled and said that it was not in his power to grant this, since even he could not bring above ground the dead who had descended to his brother's kingdom. But Zeus was so moved by the memory of the past that he went to the palace of his brother and clasping his knees asked him to accord him this favor. And the King of the Dead was greatly troubled, saying that even he who was King of the Dead could not grant this thing without involving the return to life in some difficult and painful condition. But the hero gladly accepted whatever difficult or painful condition was involved, and the King of the Dead permitted him to return not only to the earth, but to the past, and to live over again that day in all the twenty-two thousand days of his lifetime that had been least eventful; but that it must be with a mind divided into two persons,—the participant and the onlooker: the participant who does the deeds and says the words of so many years before, and the onlooker who foresees the end. So the hero returned to the sunlight and to a certain day in his fifteenth year.

"My friends," continued Chrysis, turning her eyes slowly from face to face, "as he awoke in his boyhood's room, pain filled his heart,—not only because it had started beating again, but because he saw the walls of his home and knew that in a moment he would see his parents who lay long since in the earth of that country. He descended into the courtyard. His mother lifted her eyes from the loom and greeted him and went on with her work. His father passed through the court unseeing, for on that day his mind had been full of care. Suddenly the hero saw that the living too are dead and that we can only be said to be alive in those moments when our hearts are conscious of our treasure; for our hearts are not strong enough to love every moment. And not an hour had gone by before the hero who was both watching life and living it called on Zeus to release him from so terrible a dream. The gods heard him, but before he left he fell upon the ground and kissed the soil of the world that is too dear to be realized."

It was with such eyes that Pamphilus now saw his father pass into the house and that he had seen his mother moving about, covering the fire and going about the last tasks of the day. And it was in the light of that story that his eyes had been opened to the secret life of his parents' minds. It seemed suddenly as though he saw behind the contentment and the daily talkativeness into the life of their hearts—empty, resigned, pathetic and enduring. It was Chrysis's reiterated theory of life that all human beings—save a few mysterious exceptions who seemed to be in possession of some secret from the gods—merely endured the slow misery of existence, hiding as best they could their consternation that life had no wonderful surprises after all and that its most difficult burden was the incommunicability of love. Certainly that explained the humorous sadness of his father and the fretful affection of his mother. And now as his father passed him in the courtyard this interpretation shook him more forcibly than ever. What can one do for them? What—to be equal to them—can one do for oneself? He was twenty-five already, that is—no longer a young man. He would soon be a husband and a father, a condition he did not invest with any glamour. He would soon be the head of this household and this farm. He would soon be old. Time would have flowed by him like a sigh, with no plan made, no rules set, no strategy devised that would have taught him how to save these others and himself from the creeping gray, from the too-easily accepted frustration.

"How does one live?" he asked the bright sky. "What does one do first?"

Chrysis's view of human experience expressed itself, as we have seen, in fables, in quotations from literature, in proverbs and in mottoes. Herself she summed up in a word: she regarded herself as having "died." Dead then as she was, the inconveniences of her profession, the sneers of the villagers, the ingratitude of her dependents, no longer had the power to disturb her. The only thing that troubled her in her grave was the recurrence, even in her professional associations, of a wild tenderness for this or that passerby, brief and humiliating approaches to love. These experiences and any others that were able to depress her, she now dismissed as weakness, as pride, as an old, rebellious and unwhipped vanity. The morning after the conversation with Simo at the water's edge she awoke strangely troubled; but she resolved not to examine the new dejection. It floated all day above her head,—a voice repeating: "I am alone. Why have I never seen that before? I am alone." Indeed the profession she followed was one of those that emphasize the dim notion that lies at the back of many minds: the notion that we are not necessary to anyone, that attachments weave and unweave at the mercy of separation, satiety and experience. The loneliest associations are those that pretend to intimacy.

But she had discovered two ways of mitigating this unresponsiveness and instability in the world she lived in. The first was the development she brought to the institution of the hetaira's banquet. She took endless pains over these reunions and to the wide-eyed guests they seemed indeed all that one could conceive of wit and eloquence and aristocratic ease. Great talkers are so constituted that they do not know their own thoughts until, on the tide of their particular gift, they hear them issuing from their mouths. Chrysis gave herself that luxury, the luxury of talking to these young men from her whole mind. Much of it lay beyond their reach; but her refusal to condescend, her assumption that the analysis of ideas and of masterpieces was their natural element, excited them. She knew that apart from her beauty she was not particularly fitted for her calling; she lacked the high spirits that please the customers of

middle age; but younger men, who still approach love with a touch
of awe, are not so disappointed with those common exercises when
they find them invested with melancholy, dignity and literature.
Perhaps the maturity of a civilization can be judged by this trait,
by observing whether the young men first fall in love with women
older or younger than themselves; if in their youth their imaginations pass their time in hallowing the images of prattling unnour-
ishing girls their natures will be forever after the thinner. But even
at their best Chrysis's guests seemed remote and immature to her
and finally she discovered a second way of making life more stable
and her friends more constant: she adopted stray human beings
that needed her.

In the inner monologue of her thoughts Chrysis called these
dependents her "sheep." And although they were gathered into
her shelter from places and moments of fearful extremity, they
became accustomed to their new comfort with extraordinary rapidity. In fact their past trials began to take on a romantic color and
when anything in the present situation did not suit them they had
been known to regret the lost felicities of the slave-markets, the
mills and the massacred villages. For Chrysis human nature no
longer had many surprises and the manner in which the sheep
scolded and even condescended to their shepherd did not deject
her. She loved them and was sufficiently repaid by occasional hours
of a late afternoon when the odd group would sit in the garden,
weaving in amity and humor. Such hours almost resembled life in
a home.

There was to be a banquet that evening, so shaking her head at
the shadow that hovered above her she descended into the town to
do the marketing. She was accompanied by Mysis and the porter,
—Mysis carrying a net to hold the fruit and the salad-greens, and
the porter a large jar to be filled with salt-water and then with fish

and shell-fish. Chrysis moved slowly down the long twisting flights of stairs. She was wrapped about by a great scarf of antique finely-wrinkled material and wore a broad-brimmed Tanagran hat of woven straw. The one hand that appeared outside the folds of her scarf carried a small wooden fan. It was her business to be invested with the remoteness and glamour of a legend, for at that time Greek taste turned upon a nostalgia for the antique; it was her business to be as different from other women as possible and to convert that difference into money. The shops and temporary booths were all on the open square at the water's edge and there in the bright sunlight the most excitable and loquacious of races was enjoying its morning tumult; but as this calm and day-dreaming figure appeared above them a hush fell upon the bargainers. This was the very deportment the Greek women lacked and sighed for. They were short and swarthy and shrill, and their incessant conversation was accompanied by the incessant play of their hands. The whole race was haunted by a passionate admiration for poise and serenity and slow motion, and now for an hour the Andrian's every move was followed by the furtive glances of the islanders, with mingled awe and hatred. The Brynians, when she appeared, felt themselves to be provincial and commercial. From time to time some of the young men who had been guests at her house approached her and spoke to her. Then it was that the unmarried girls and the young wives of the island gazed with consternation and fallen jaw at the way she smiled and talked and dismissed their brothers and their future husbands. Philumena, in the shadow of an awning, leaned back against a wall and watched the stranger; turning her head slightly she could see Pamphilus at the tally-desk in the door of his father's warehouse. Her eyes fell on her rough gown and her red arms and a long slow blush mounted to her face. But all the while Chrysis's heart had been growing heavier. "I have lived alone and I shall die alone," it said, and groaned within her.

As she returned to her house from the market she fell into a feverish monologue. "The fault is in me. It's my lack of perseverance in affection. I know that. Now, Chrysis, you must begin your life over again; you must assemble some plan. You must devote yourself with all your mind to your sheep. You must break down all their coldness and wilfulness. You must make yourself love them again. You must bring back the happiness you felt with each one of them when you first knew them. It is routine, it is the daily contact that has spoiled all that. It's cowardly of me to be able to love people only when they are new. Now, now, Chrysis!—arise!" For the hundredth time she was visited by hope and courage. She would win in this thing. As she approached the house she was all but stumbling in her eagerness; she would create a home. "If I love them enough, I can understand them," she muttered. "One never learns how to live, or one's lights on living arrive too late, when one has spoiled the surrounding situation, spoiled it beyond repair. But I am to be on the earth for fifty years, and I must do it."

Chrysis did not realize what took place in the house during her absences, and that when she left it the house was empty. The personalities of her flock were extinguished. They fretted; they hovered about the gates peering in the direction from which she would return, and their minds ceased to act save in terms of that resentment which is the complement of devotion. She did not realize that this wasting of love in fretfulness was one of the principal activities on the planet. When she was away fear descended upon them; their dependence upon her was so great that even her temporary absences reminded them of the destitution from which they had been lifted,—circumstances so fearful that their conscious minds never revisited them, but which hovered in the distance enriching their present ease and hardening their self-centredness. All this antagonism therefore met her in a flood as she stumbled across the threshold of her home. By the middle of the afternoon she was saying to herself, almost in a panic: "It is impossible. I can do nothing. They even hate me. But fortunately I am dead. It is not my pride that is hurt. I am at peace in the ground. Yet oh! if only we had some help in these matters. If only the gods were sometimes present among us. To have nothing to go by except this idea, this vague idea, that there lies the principle of living!"

During the banquet she looked about her for comfort. "It is also cowardly of me to be happy only at the banquets where I can lead the conversation and display my thoughts and be admired." But tonight even that exhilaration was wanting; her guests seemed younger and remoter then ever, and she in turn was capricious and all but irritable. It was to be expected, therefore, that the conversation would take turns little likely to comfort her.

Niceratus, one of the more assured of her guests, asked her what life would be like in two thousand years.

"Why," she said at once, "there will be no more war."

"I should not wish to be alive in a world where there was no war," he replied. "That would be an age of women."

Now Chrysis was jealous of the dignity of women and lost no occasions to combat such hasty disparagements. She leaned forward and asked encouragingly:

"You wish to serve the state, Niceratus?"

"I do."

"And you admire courage?"

"I do, Chrysis."

"Then go bear children," she replied, turning away.

Niceratus found this remark unseemly and left the house. (He absented himself from the two successive banquets, but later returned and asked her pardon for making a personal grievance out of a difference of opinion. Confessions of error always gave Chrysis great pleasure. "Happy are the associations," she would say, "that have grown out of a fault and a forgiveness.")

The conversation then turned upon the plays concerning Medea and Phaedra which she had read to them at an earlier banquet and upon all manifestations of extravagant passion. The young men declared that the problem was not as complicated as it appeared to be and that such women should have been whipped like disobedient slaves and shut up in a room with a jar of water and a little plain food until their pride was subdued. They then recounted to her, almost in whispers, the story of a girl from a village on the further side of the island whose behavior had thrown her family and her friends into consternation. The girl had continued for a time, glorying in her disorders, until one morning, rising early, she had climbed a high cliff near her home and thrown herself into the sea. A silence fell on the company as all turned inquiringly to Chrysis asking for the explanation of such a reversal.

To herself she said: "Do not try to explain to them. Talk of other things. Stupidity is everywhere and invincible." But their continued expectancy prevailed upon her. She seemed to struggle with herself for a moment, deeply troubled, and then began in a low voice: "Once upon a time the great army of women came together to a meeting. And they invited to this meeting one man, a tragic poet. They told him that they wished to send a message to the world of men and that he was to be their advocate and mouthpiece. 'Tell them,' said the women eagerly, 'that it is only in appearance that we are unstable. Tell them that this is because we are hard-pressed and in bitter servitude to nature, but that at heart, only asking their patience, we are as steadfast, as brave and as manly as they.' The poet smiled sadly, saying that the men who knew this already would merely be ashamed to be told it again, and the men who did not know it would learn nothing through the mere telling; but he consented to deliver the message. The men at first were silent, then one by one they broke out into laughter. And they sent the poet back to the army of women with these words: 'Tell them not to be anxious and not to trouble their pretty heads with these matters. Tell them that their popularity is not dying out, and let them not endanger it through heroics.' When the poet had repeated these words to the women, some blushed with shame and some with anger; some rose with a weary sigh: 'We should never have spoken to them,' they said. They went back to their mirrors and started combing their hair and as they combed their hair they wept."

Chrysis had barely finished this story when a young man who had hitherto taken little part in the conversation suddenly launched into a violent condemnation of her means of livelihood. This youth was of that temper that seeks to mould the lives of others abruptly to certain patterns of its own choosing. He now commanded Chrysis to become a servant or a sempstress. The other guests began to whisper among themselves and to avert their faces from confusion and anger, but Chrysis sat gazing at his flashing eyes and admiring his earnestness. There was a certain luxury in having an external mortification added to an inner despair. She was already troubled by her recent discomfiture of Niceratus and now chose to be magnanimous. She arose and approached the

young fanatic; taking his hand she smiled at him with grave affection, saying to the company: "It is true that of all forms of genius,
goodness has the longest awkward age."

But these incidents were not of a nature to distract her mind
from the protracted oppression of the day. "Vain. Empty. Transi-
tory," the voice within her repeated. But just as she was about to
finish the day with the comprehensive summary that she had
nothing to lend to life and no place to fill, her eyes fell upon
Pamphilus. It was his custom, through lack of self-confidence, to
take the last seat at the remote end of the room. The guests
acknowledged his preëminence among them, but when one evening they had wished to elect him King of the Banquet he had
furtively and savagely intimated to them his refusal and the votes
had passed to another. But Chrysis's eyes had often, as now, rested
upon that head bent forward to receive her every word and that
received each one with so earnest a frown.

"That is something!" she said to herself suddenly and for a
moment her heart stopped beating.

She had intended to recite to them *The Clouds* of Aristophanes
that evening, but she now changed her mind. She felt the need to
nourish her heart and those watchful eyes with something lofty
and deeply felt. Perhaps what she called the "lofty" was in this
world merely a beautiful form of falsehood, cheating the heart.
But she would try again tonight and see whether, after so dejected
a day, it woke any stir of conviction. "What shall I read?" she
asked herself as the tables were being removed. "Something from
Homer?—Priam begging of Achilles the body of Hector? No.
. . . No. . . . Nor would they understand the *Oedipus at Colonus. The Alcestis? The Alcestis?*"

One of the shyer guests, seeing her deliberating over the choice

of the evening's declamation, timidly asked her to read the *Phaedrus* of Plato.

"Oh, my friend," she said, "I have not seen the book for several
years. I should be obliged to improvise long stretches in it. . . ."

"Could you . . . could you read the opening and the close?"

"I shall try it for you," she replied and rising slowly disposed
the folds of her robe about her. The servants withdrew and silence
fell upon the company. This was the moment (on happier evenings) that she loved; this hush, this eagerness, this faintly mocking affection. What drives them—she would ask herself—in the
next fifteen years to become so graceless . . . so pompous, or
envious, or so busily cheerful?

At first all went well. The boys listened with delight to the
account of how other young men gathered in the streets and
palaestra of Athens to hear the arguments of Socrates. Listening,
they agreed that nothing in the world was more to be prized than a
beautifully ordered speech. Then followed the description of the
walk that Socrates and Phaedrus took into the country. *"This is
indeed a rare resting-place. This plane-tree is not only tall, but
thick and spreading. And this agnus castus is at the very moment
of flowering and its shade and its fragrance will render our stay the
more agreeable. These images and these votive-offerings tell us
that the place is surely sacred to some nymphs and to some river-
god. . . . Truly, Phaedrus, you are an admirable guide."*

From there she passed to the close:

"But let us go now, as the heat of the day is over.

*"Socrates: Would it not be well before we go to offer up a
prayer to the gods of this place?*

"Phaedrus: It would, Socrates.

*"Socrates: Beloved Pan, and all ye other gods who haunt this
place, grant that I may become beautiful in the inner man and may*

whatever I possess without be in harmony with that which is
within. May I esteem the wise men alone to be rich. And may my
store of gold be such as none but the good may bear. Phaedrus,
need we say anything more? As for myself I have prayed enough.

"*Phaedrus: And let the same prayer serve for me, for these are*
the things friends share with one another."

All went well until this phrase. Then Chrysis, the serene, the
happily dead, seeing the tears that stood in the eyes of Pamphilus,
could go no further, and before them all she wept as one weeps
who after an absence of folly and self-will returns to a well-loved
place and an old loyalty. It was true, true beyond a doubt, tragi-
cally true, that the world of love and virtue and wisdom was the
true world and her failure in it all the more overwhelming. But
she was not alone; he too saw the long and failing war as she did,
and she loved him as though she were loving for the first time and
as one is never able to love again. That was sealed; that was
forever assigned.

After a few moments she collected herself and quieted the
guests who had risen in concern about her. "Sit down, my friends.
I am ready now," she said smiling. "I shall read you *The Clouds*
of Aristophanes."

But it was some time before the laughter rose among the
couches, the laughter that was a just tribute to the divine wit of the
poet of *The Clouds*.

Brynos rose with the dawn, and it was not many hours later that
the morning's work was over. Several days after the conversation
recorded above, Pamphilus, having helped his father in the warehouse and being in no mood for exercising in the field, started out
to walk to the highest point on the island. It was early Spring. A
strong wind had blown every cloud from the sky and the sea lay

covered with flying white-tipped waves. His garments leapt and
billowed about him and his very hair tugged at his head. The gulls
themselves, leaning upon the gusts, were caught unawares from
time to time and blown with ruffled feathers and scandalized cries
towards the violet-blue zenith. Pamphilus led his life with much
worry and self-examination and all the exhilaration of wind and
sun could not drive from his mind the anxious affection with
which he now turned over his thoughts of Chrysis and Philumena
and of the four members of his family. He was straying among the
rocks and the lizards and the neglected dwarfed olive-trees, when
his attention was suddenly caught by an incident on the hillside to
his left. A group of boys from the town was engaged in tormenting a young girl. She was retreating backwards up the slope
through a disused orchard, shouting haughtily back at her pur-
suers. The boys' malice had turned to anger; they were retorting
hotly and letting fly about her a few harmless stones. Pamphilus
strode over to the group and with a gesture ordered the boys down
the hill. The girl, her face still flushed and distrustful, stood with
her back against a tree and waited for him to come toward her.
They looked at one another for a moment in silence. Finally
Pamphilus said:

"What is the matter?"

"They're just country fools, that's all. They've never seen anyone before who didn't come from their wretched Brynos." And
then from rage and disappointment she began to cry uncontrollably and despairingly.

Pamphilus watched her for a time and then asked her where she
had been going.

"Nowhere. I was just going for a walk and they followed me
from the town. I can't do anything. I can't go anywhere. . . . I
wasn't hurting them. I was just going for a walk alone and they

called names after me. They followed me way up here; I called
names at them and then they started throwing things at me. That's
all."

"I thought I knew everyone on the island," said Pamphilus
thoughtfully, "but I have never seen you before. Have you been
here long?"

"Yes, I've been here almost a year," she replied, adding indis-
tinctly, ". . . but I hardly ever go out or anything."

"You hardly ever go out?"

"No," and she fumbled with her dress and stared at the sea,
frowning.

"You should try to know some of the other girls and go out for
walks with them."

This time she turned and looked into his face. "I don't know
any of the other girls. I . . . I live at home and they don't let me
go out of the house, except when I go out for walks nights with
. . . well, with Mysis." She continued to be shaken with sobs, but
she was adjusting her hair and the folds of her dress. "I don't see
why they have to throw stones at me," she added.

Pamphilus looked at her in silence, gravely. Presently he collected himself and said: "There's a big smooth stone over there.
Will you go over there and sit down?"

She followed him to the stone, still busy with her hair and
drawing her fingers across her eyes and cheeks.

"I have a sister just about your age," said Pamphilus. "You can
begin by knowing her. You can go for walks with her and then
you wouldn't be a stranger any more. Her name is Argo. You'd
like one another, I know. My sister is weaving a large mantle for
my mother and she'd like you to help her with it and she could
help you with yours. Are you making a mantle?"

"Yes."

"That would be fine," said Pamphilus, and from that moment Glycerium loved him forever.

"I probably know your father, don't I?" he asked.

"I have no father," she replied, looking up at him weakly, "I am the sister of the woman from Andros."

"Oh . . . oh . . .," said Pamphilus, more astonished than he had ever been in his life. "I know your sister well."

"Yes," said Glycerium. Her bright wet eyes strayed over the streaked sea and the blown birds. "She doesn't want anyone to know that I'm there. All day I stay up on the top of the house or work in the court. Only at night I'm allowed to go for a walk with Mysis. Even now I'm supposed to be in the house, but I broke my promise. She has gone to the market and so I broke my promise. I wanted to see what the island and the sea look like by day. And I wanted to look across to Andros where I come from. But the boys followed me here and threw stones at me and I can never come again."

Here she fell to weeping even more despairingly than before and Pamphilus could do nothing but say "Well" several times and "Yes." At last he asked her what her name was.

"Glycerium. Chrysis went away from home a long time ago and I was living with my brother and he died and I couldn't live with him any more. And I had nowhere to go or anything, and one day she came back and took me to live with her. That's all."

"Have you any brothers or sisters?"

"Oh, no."

"Who is Mysis?"

"Mysis isn't Greek. She is from Alexandria. Chrysis found her. All of them in the house,—she just found them somewhere. That's what she does. Mysis was a slave in the cloth mills. Sometimes she tells me about it."

Pamphilus still gazed at her, and bringing back her wandering evasive glance from the sea she looked at him from her thin face and enormous hungry eyes. Even a long glance did not now embarrass them.

"Do you want me to ask Chrysis to let you go about the island by day?" he asked.

"If she doesn't want it, we mustn't change her. Chrysis knows best." She turned away from him and said in a lower voice, dreamy and embittered: "But what can become of me? Am I always to stay locked up? I am fifteen already. The world is full of wonderful things and people that I might never know about. I know it was wrong of me to break my promise; but to live for years without ever knowing new people,—to hear them passing the door all day, and to see them a long ways off. Do you think I did very wrong?"

"No."

"I don't know anyone. I don't know anyone."

"Well . . . well, you'll come to know my sister. That will be a beginning," he said, taking her fingertips thoughtfully and wonderingly in his.

"Yes," she said.

"Everything is beginning over again. I'm your friend. Then my sister. Soon you will have a great many. You'll see."

"But where will I be five years from now and ten years from now," she cried, staring about her wildly. "I don't know. I'm afraid. I'm unhappy. Everyone in the world is happy except me."

The caress of the hands in first love, and never so simply again, seems to be a sharing of courage, an alliance of two courages against a confusing world. As his hand passed from her hair to her shoulder, she turned to him with parted lips and hesitant eyes, then suddenly bound both her arms about his neck. Into his ears her lips wildly and all but meaninglessly repeated: "Yes. Yes. Yes. I can't stay there forever. I should never know anyone. I should never see anybody."

"She will let you come to see me," he said.

"No," said Glycerium. "But I'll come by myself. I mustn't ask her. She would not let me come. She always knows best. And the boys can throw their stones. I don't mind if you're here. What . . . what is your name?"

"My name is Pamphilus, Glycerium."

"Can . . . can I call you by it?"

It was not at this meeting, nor at their next, but at the third, beneath the dwarfed olive-trees, that those caresses that seemed to be for courage, for pity and for admiration, were turned by Nature to her own uses.

These conversations took place in the early Spring. One afternoon in the late Summer Chrysis slipped out of her house and climbed the hill behind it. She was filled with a great desire to be alone and to think. She looked out over the glittering sea. The winds were moderate on that afternoon and before them the innumerable neat waves hurried toward the shore, running up the sands with a long whisper, or discreetly lifting against the rocks a scarf of foam. In the distance a school of dolphins engaged at their eternal games led the long procession of curving backs. The water was marbled at intervals with the strange fields and roadways of a lighter blue; and behind all she beheld with love the violet profile of Andros. For a time she strayed about upon the crest of the hill, making sure that no one was watching or following her, then descending the further side she sought out her favorite retreats, a point of rock that projected into the sea and a sheltered cove beside it. As she drew near the place, she stumbled forward, almost run-

ning, and as she went she murmured soothingly to herself: "We
are almost there. Look, we are almost there now." At last,
climbing over the boulders she let herself down into an amphitheatre of hot dry sand. She started unbinding her hair, but
stopped herself abruptly: "No, no. I must think. I should fall
asleep here. I must think first. I shall come back soon," she muttered to the amphitheatre, and continuing her journey she reached
the furthermost heap of stones and sat down. She rested her chin
upon her hand and fixing her eyes upon the horizon she waited for
the thoughts to come.

The first thing to think about was her new illness. Several times
she had been awakened by a wild fluttering in her left side that
continued, deepening, until it seemed to her as though a great
stake were being driven into her heart. And all the day the sensation would remain with her as of a heavy object burdening the place
where this trouble lay. "Probably . . . very likely," she said to
herself, "the next time I shall die of it." At the thought a wave of
anticipation passed over her. "I shall probably die of it," she repeated cheerfully and became interested in some crayfish in the
pool at her feet. She plucked some grasses behind her and started
dragging them before the eyes of the indignant animals. "Nothing
in life could make me abandon my sheep, but if I die they will
have to fall back on Circumstance as I did. Glycerium, what will
become of you? Apraxine, Mysis . . .? There are times when we
cannot see one step ahead of us, but five years later we are eating
and sleeping somewhere." (It was humorous, pretending that
one's heart was as hard as that.) "Yes," she said aloud, to the pain
that trembled within her, "only come quickly." She leaned forward still dragging the stems before the shellfish: "I have lived
thirty-five years. I have lived enough. *Stranger, near this spot lies
Chrysis, daughter of Arches of Andros: the ewe that has strayed*

from the flock lives many years in one day and dies at a great age when the sun sets." She laughed at the deceptive comforts of self-pity and taking off a sandal put her foot into the water. She drew herself up for a moment, asking herself what there was left in the house for the colony's supper; then recollecting some fish and some salad on the shelf, she returned to her thoughts. She repeated her epitaph, making it a song and emphasizing, for self-mockery, its false sentiment. "O Andros, O Poseidon, how happy I am. I have no right to be happy like this. . . ."

And she knew as she gazed at the frieze of dolphins still playing in the distance that her mind was avoiding another problem that awaited her. "I am happy because I love this Pamphilus,— Pamphilus the anxious, Pamphilus the stupid. Why cannot some- one tell him that it is not necessary to suffer so about living." And the low exasperated sigh escaped her, the protest we make at the preposterous, the incorrigible beloved. "He thinks he is failing. He thinks he is inadequate to life at every turn. Let him rest some day, O ye Olympians, from pitying those who suffer. Let him learn to look the other way. This is something new in the world, this concern for the unfit and the broken. Once he begins that, there's no end to it, only madness. It leads nowhere. That is some god's business." Whereupon she discovered that she was weeping; but when she had dried her eyes she was still thinking about him. "Oh, such people are unconscious of their goodness. They strike their foreheads with their hands because of their failure, and yet the rest of us are made glad when we remember their faces. Pam- philus, you are another herald from the future. Some day men will be like you. Do not frown so. . . ."

But these thoughts were very fatiguing. She arose and, returning to the amphitheatre, laid herself down upon the sand. She mur- mured some fragments from the Euripidean choruses and fell asleep. She had always been an islander and this hot and impersonal sun playing upon a cold and impersonal sea was not unfriendly to her. And now for two hours the monotony of sun and sea played about her and wove itself into the mood of her sleeping mind. As once the gray-eyed Athena stood guarding Ulysses—she leaning upon her spear, her great heart full of concern and of those long divine thoughts that are her property—even so, now, the hour and the place all but gathered itself into a presence and shed its influence upon her. When her eyes finally opened she listened for a time to the calm in her heart. "Some day," she said, "we shall understand why we suffer. I shall be among the shades underground and some wonderful hand, some Alcestis, will touch me and will show me the meaning of all these things; and I shall laugh softly for hours as I do now . . . as I do now."

She arose and binding up her hair prepared to ascend the slope. But just as she turned to leave the place, there visited her the desire to do something ceremonial, to mark the hour. She stood up straightly and held out her arms to the setting sun: "If you still hear prayers from the lips of mortals, if our longings touch you at all, hear me now. Give to this Pamphilus some assurance—even some assurance such as you have given to me, unstable though I am—that he is right. And oh! (but I do not say this from vanity or pride, O Apollo,—but perhaps this is weak, this is childish of me, perhaps this renders the whole prayer powerless!) if it is possible, let the thought of me or of something I have said be comforting to him some day. And . . . and . . ."

But her arms fell to her side. The world seemed empty. The sun went down. The sea and sky became suddenly remote and she was left with only the tears in her eyes and the longing in her heart. She closed her lips and turned her head aside. "I suppose there is no god," she whispered. "We must do these things ourselves. We must drag ourselves through life as best we can."

Chrysis had made the mistake of accustoming the members of her household to her invariable presence and now while she slept they became increasingly indignant at the length of her absence. In twos and threes they hovered about the door peering to the right and to the left with mingled scorn and alarm.

"When she comes in, see that no one says a word to her," directed Apraxine, a tall lame woman whom Chrysis had found beaten and left for dead at the edge of the desert below the terraces of Alexandria.

"Pretend you don't see her."

". . . to go sallying off a whole day without a word to a soul."

"I'm sure I don't wish to stay in a house where I count for nothing."

". . . less than nothing, it seems."

Presently however something happened that distracted their minds from their resentment. A new sheep arrived at the fold.

Simo's frank had carried to Andros the money that Chrysis intended for the support of the stricken sea-captain. But Philocles's guardians had long since tired of their charge and become discontented with the intermittent payments. They decided to take advantage of this sum of money to ship him off to Brynos. It was necessary for this purpose to wait for a lucid interval in the patient's condition. Such a moment finally arrived; they hurriedly made up his bundle, brushed his hair, and led him down to the waterfront, where they found the captain of a boat sailing between the Cyclades who was willing to undertake the commission. And thus it was that on the afternoon of Chrysis's retreat to solitude

Philocles arrived on Brynos. A boy who attended at one of the wine-shops in the town was directed to escort him to her house, and suddenly the childlike sea-captain was thrust into the courtyard among the conspiring pensioners.

Ten years before Philocles had been the greatest navigator on the Mediterranean, first in skill and experience and first in fame. He had been many times to Sicily and to Carthage; he had passed through the Gates of Hercules and visited the Tyrian mines in Britain. He had sailed westward for months across the great shelf of water, seeking new islands, and had been forced to turn back by the visible anger of the gods. In the present age men were captains or merchants or farmers, but in the great age men had been first Athenians or Greeks, and the islanders regarded Philocles as of that order, a belated giant. He was already in middle life when Chrysis first knew him—she had been a passenger on one of his trips to Egypt—and it astonished her to find someone laconic in a chattering world and with quiet hands in a gesturing civilization. He was blackened and cured by all weathers. He stood in the squares of the various ports of call, his feet apart as though they were forever planted on a shifting deck. He seemed to be too large for daily life; his very eyes were strange—unaccustomed to the shorter range, too used to seizing the appearances of a constellation between a cloud and a cloud, and the outlines of a headland in rain. Wind, salt and starvation had moulded his head, and his mind had been rendered, not buoyant, but rich and concentrated by the enforced asceticisms of a prolonged duty and of long sea voyages. He had been one of the persons whom Chrysis had most loved in all her life and it was she who had discovered his secret, the secret that it was neither adventure nor gain that drove him along his adventurous life. He was passing the time and filling the hours in anticipation of release from a life that had lost its savor with the death of his daughter. These two saw in one another's eyes the thing they had in common, the fact that they had both died to themselves. They lived at one remove from that self that supports the generality of men, the self that is a bundle of self-assertions, of greeds, of vanities and of easily-offended pride. Three years before, Philocles had been forced to captain some ships of a city at war. He had been captured and mutilated and what was left of so kingly a person was a timorous child.

The sheep examined the newcomer who had been thrust so abruptly into their midst. They questioned him and amused themselves with his answers. Then they gave him a bench in the sunlight where he might whisper to his heart's content.

The sun set and soon after Chrysis came stumbling through the door, laughing apologetically and pushing back her hair. "Forgive me, O my dear friends, forgive me. I fell asleep on the sand and I'm very sorry I'm so late." (The men and women raised their eyebrows cynically and went on with their work.) "Apraxine, has anything happened?" (Apraxine cleared her throat with Alexandrian hauteur and became absorbed in looking for a thread on the ground.) "Now we must find something particularly rare for supper."

The sheep exchanged pitying glances over all this tawdry artifice and when Chrysis passed into the house they burst into laughter. The laughter was condescending, but the soul had returned to the community. Finally at a signal from Apraxine, Glycerium went to the door and announced to Chrysis that Philocles had arrived from Andros. He had seen her pass and some twinge of memory had set him trembling. He rose and walked unsteadily to the middle of the court. She saw him standing before her, haggard, with hollow puzzled eyes and with untrimmed beard.

She went forward repeating, "My dear friend, my friend!" but as she embraced him a loud voice within her seemed to say: "Something is going to happen. The threads of my life are drawing together."

That night Chrysis was awakened from a light and feverish sleep by the instinctive knowledge that someone was near her. She raised herself on one elbow and peered toward the faint glimmer of the door.

"Who is it? Who is there?" she said.

A figure seemed suddenly to rise from the threshold. "It's I, Chrysis. It's Glycerium."

"Is something the matter? Is someone ill?"

"No . . . it's only . . ."

"Light a lamp, my child. What do you want?"

"Chrysis, are you angry with me for waking you up? I couldn't sleep, Chrysis, and I had to come into your room."

"But why are you crying, my dear, my dove? Come now and sit on the edge of the bed. Of course I'm not angry with you." Glycerium sank upon the floor beside her. "No, no,—the floor is cold. Come sit up here. Your hair is wet! Tell me now, what is making you unhappy?"

"Nothing."

"What? Then you have something to tell me?"

"No . . . I don't know what . . . I just want you to talk to me."

"Well, I have something to tell you." Chrysis was stroking Glycerium's hair, delicately following with her finger-tips the strands as they passed above and behind the ear, when suddenly Glycerium threw her arms about her sister's neck and sobbed uncontrollably. Chrysis continued gravely with her caress, thinking that she was merely dealing with one of the meaningless accesses of despair that descend upon adolescence when the slow ache of existence is first apprehended by the growing mind. "There!" she murmured in a rhythmic undertone, "Sh . . . sh . . . sh . . . sh. . . . We love you. We all love you in this house. Our beautiful Glycerium, our gentle, our very beautiful Glycerium . . . sh . . . sh . . . there! Are you comfortable now? I have some good news for you. (No, no, there is plenty of room.) This is it: Beginning tomorrow you are going to lead an altogether different life. I am going to let you wander all over the island alone. And when Mysis and I go to market you can go with us. You may climb the hills if you like, and you may explore along the water's edge,—I shall even show you the secret of the secrets of my heart,—a beautiful hidden shelter by the sea where one can be perfectly alone. . . . Well? are you pleased? Doesn't this news make you happy?"

"Yes, Chrysis."

"Now! I thought it would make you very happy and all you say is: Yes, Chrysis!"

"Chrysis, tell me: what will become of me?"

Chrysis changed her position and in the dark shut her eyes a moment. "Oh, my dear, my dear . . . that's what everyone asks, everyone on earth. Well, first you tell me: what do you want to become?"

"I want to marry someone and . . . and be in his home. Chrysis, tell me: can I marry someone? Without a father and a mother and without anything, is it possible that I can marry someone?"

"My dear, there is always . . ."

"Chrysis, I'm grown-up now. I'm fifteen. Please tell me the truth. I must know. Don't say something merely to quiet me. I must know the truth. Can a man ever ask me to marry him? Why are you waiting so long to answer me?"

"I have been planning to have a long talk with you about all these things. But not now. Wait a short time; wait until you have had a week, two weeks, of this new life when you will be free to wander all over the island. Then you will be able to understand better what I have to say."

Glycerium paused a moment. "I know, I know," she said, her face against Chrysis's shoulder. "That means that no one will ever be able to marry me."

"No, no, I don't say that. . . ."

Glycerium rose and stood in the middle of the room. "I understand," she said in the darkness.

Chrysis raised herself again on one elbow and said slowly: "We are not Greek citizens. We are not people with homes. We are considered strange, only a little above the slaves. All those others live in homes and everyone knows their fathers and their mothers; they marry one another. They think we would never fit into their life. Although all that is true,—"

"But there are stories," said Glycerium, "of men who even married girls that had been slaves."

"Yes, if a young man should fall in love with you, it is possible that he would take you into his home. That is why I have tried to take such care of you and why I have kept you hidden here in the house. Through the young men who come to the banquets, the island knows that you are here and that you have been carefully protected. And now that you are to walk about the island freely you must be a hundred times more careful than other girls. You are beautiful and you are good, and before all their unfriendly eyes you must show them your modesty and your goodness. That is all there is to say and to hope, my child."

"Perhaps, Chrysis . . . it is best that I do not go about the island freely, after all."

"No, no. You will feel like going out. It will come gradually. But now you must go to bed and to sleep, my darling. All these things will solve themselves as best they can. All you can do for the present is to be yourself, your very self, my Glycerium."

Glycerium moved unsteadily towards the bed: "Chrysis, I must tell you something."

"Yes? . . ."

"You will be angry with me, Chrysis."

"Why . . ."

"May the gods protect me, I . . . I have been talking with Mysis and now I know that I am going to be the mother of a child."

There was silence for a moment followed by the sound of Chrysis putting her feet upon the floor. "Where is Mysis? Let me get up."

"It is true, Chrysis. I broke my promise the times when you were away. I used to go out over the hills."

"Oh, my child, my child!"

"But he loves me. He will marry me. He loves me, I know."

"Who is it? What is his name?"

"It is Pamphilus, son of Simo."

Chrysis grew rigid in the darkness. Then she slowly put her feet back into the bed. Glycerium continued wildly: "He loves me. He will take care of me. He has told me so a hundred times. Chrysis, what shall I do? What shall I do? I am afraid."

A low moan at the door revealed the fact that Mysis had accompanied her younger mistress to this interview and was kneeling outside the door without the courage to enter.

After a moment Chrysis said in a light impersonal voice: "Well, you . . . go off to bed now and go to sleep. Yes. We'll both be catching cold here. It's late. I think it must be almost morning."

"I cannot sleep."

"Everything will be all right, Glycerium. I can't talk any more now. I'm not well. We'll talk about it in the morning."

Glycerium left the room, trembling.

In her darker hours Chrysis carried on what she called a "dialogue with Fate." And now as she turned to the wall she said: "I hear you. You have won again."

Before long the pain in her side became fixed and unremitting, and Chrysis knew that her life was drawing to a close. She took to her bed and her thoughts no longer clung to the world about her. Now when her courage was being undermined by her pain she dared not ask herself if she had lived and if she were dying, unloved, in disorder, without meaning. From time to time she peered into her mind to ascertain what her beliefs were in regard to a life after death, its judgments or its felicities; but the most exhausting of all our adventures is that journey down the long corridors of the mind to the last halls where belief is enthroned. She resigned herself to the memory of certain moments when intuition had comforted her and she quieted her heart with Andrian cradle-songs and with fragments from the tragic poets. She saved her strength to fulfill a last desire, one that may perhaps seem unworthy to persons of a later age. Her mind had been moulded by formal literature, by epics and odes, by tragedies and by heroic biography, and from this reading she had been imbued with the superstition that one should die in a noble manner, and in this high decorum even the maintenance of her beauty played a part. The only terror left in the world was the fear that she might leave it with cries of pain, with a torn mind, and with discomposed features.

The news spread about the island that the Andrian was gravely ill. The young men who had been her guests were confused by the discrepancy between their mothers' sarcasms and the respect that Chrysis had inspired in themselves, but some brought shy offerings of wine and cheese to her door. For such brief interviews she raised herself on one elbow and sought to recover her light-spoken graciousness. But most of the young men stayed away; it required a maturer mind than they could summon to hold side by side their memories of sensual pleasure and their respect due to the dying.

Pamphilus had other reasons for staying away. It seemed more and more unlikely that he would ever be permitted to marry Glycerium. But one morning he appeared at Chrysis's house and asked to see her. He traversed the court, picking his way among her motley and dismayed pensioners, and his eyes fell upon Glycerium. She was seated beside Philocles at her sister's door, silent and without hope. Pamphilus stopped for a moment on one knee before her and took her hands in his. "Do not be afraid," he said in a low voice. "No harm will come to you." She derived no courage from his words; she lifted her eyes and scanned his face. Her mouth trembled, but no words came and her eyes returned to the ground. Pamphilus passed into the room where Chrysis lay; for a moment he could distinguish nothing in the darkness. Presently he became aware of the priest of Aesculapius and Apollo bending over a brazier in the corner, and finally he saw Chrysis smiling at him gravely from the bed. He sat down beside her in silence; each waited for the other to begin.

"We are sorry, all of us are sorry, Chrysis," he said at last, "to hear that you have been so ill."

"Thank you, Pamphilus. Thank them all."

"There . . . there has been so much rain. When the sunlight returns you will feel better at once."

"Yes, it has always been the sunlight that has done me the most good. You are all well on your farm?"

"Yes, the gods be praised."

"The gods be praised. I shall never forget a favor your father did for me."

Pamphilus was struck with amazement. "My father?"

"Oh, forgive me . . . I remember now I promised him not to mention it to you. Oh, my illness has made me forget that. I am ashamed, I am ashamed. But now I had better add that it was a small commission he did for me by one of his boats going to Andros. I would not have him think me unfaithful to my promise. I beg of you earnestly not to tell him that I spoke of it."

"Indeed, I shall not tell him, Chrysis."

There fell another pause between them, while her strengthless hands lightly pressed upon the bed in her self-reproach.

"Yes," said Pamphilus. "When there is more sunlight you will feel better at once. The sky has been overcast for a long time. I cannot remember when it has been overcast so long."

To themselves they both cried: "How shall we ever get out of this?"

"We have missed the banquets. I would like to tell you again, Chrysis, what great pleasure they gave me. I have been looking forward to the next one when you promised to read us I forget what play."

"It was to have been the *Ion* of Euripides."

"Yes."

"This," said Chrysis, glancing toward the priest with a smile, "this is my Ion."

But perhaps the words were ill-chosen. She thought she saw the priest frowning as he bent over his work. "Forgive me," she said to him abruptly, "if I have offended you. I did not mean it ill."

But the tears were rolling down her cheeks. "Life, Pamphilus," she said, "is full of mistakes, but the wrongs we do to those we

love and honor are more than we can endure." The priest approached the further side of the bed and adjusted the pillows; he
whispered a few words into her ear and went back to his brazier.

"Am I tiring you?" Pamphilus asked.

"No, no. I am very happy that you have come." To herself she
thought: "Time is passing, and what are we saying! Is there not
something heartfelt that I can find to say to him, something to
remember, for him and for me?" But she distrusted the emotion
that filled her heart. It was perhaps mere excitement and pain; or a
vague and false sentiment. Probably the best thing to do was to be
stoic; to be brave and inarticulate; to talk of trivial things. Or was
it a greater bravery to surmount this shame and to say whatever
obvious words the heart dictated? Which was right?

Pamphilus was thinking: "She is dying. What can I say to her?
But I have never been able to place words rightly. I am dull. I am
nothing to her but the man who has wronged her sister." Aloud he
said in a low voice: "I shall marry Glycerium if I can, Chrysis. At
all events you may be sure that no harm will come to her."

"Though I love her dearly," replied Chrysis, finding her words
with great difficulty, "I shall not urge you. I . . . I no longer
believe that what happens to us is important. You will marry
Glycerium or another. The years will unfold these things. It is the
life in the mind that is important."

"I shall do what I can for her."

"You have only to be yourself without fear, without doubting,
Pamphilus."

"Chrysis, you will forgive me for having spoken to you so little
at the banquets . . . and for having sat at the further end and
. . . that is the way I am. It was not because I did not respect you.
I cannot talk as those others can. I am only a listener. Even now I
cannot say what I mean. But I followed all that you said."

The pain in Chrysis's side seemed to increase beyond all endurance. "Oh, friend," she said, "do not distrust. These things are not so unsatisfactory . . . so interrupted as they seem to be." The priest had been watching her; she made a slight sign to him. "I do not wish you to go away," she continued to Pamphilus, almost in a whisper, "but it is best that I sleep now." Then raising herself on one elbow she breathed in anguish: "Perhaps we shall meet somewhere beyond life when all these pains shall have been removed. I think the gods have some mystery still in store for us. But if we do not, let me say now . . ." her hands opened and closed upon the cloths that covered her, ". . . I want to say to someone . . . that I have known the worst that the world can do to me, and that nevertheless I praise the world and all living. All that is, is well. Remember some day, remember me as one who loved all things and accepted from the gods all things, the bright and the dark. And do you likewise. Farewell."

Simo arose early to witness Chrysis's funeral. The Greeks, for reasons that lay deep in their sense of the fitness of things and in their superstition, conducted their funerals in the hour before dawn, and it was therefore still profound night when the little procession of her household prepared to pass through the streets of the town. When Simo arrived at the square he found that many of the men of Brynos had already gathered there and, drawing the folds of their rough cloaks about them, were standing talking together in low voices. The men of his own age had brought their curiosity and contempt with them and were congratulating themselves on the island's happy deliverance from the foreign woman; but the younger men who had known Chrysis stood with sullen faces, their throats rigid with antagonism at the glee of their elders. Simo took his place in silence beside Chremes, but refused to respond to the latter's animated comment. Presently as the sounds of the flute and the mourners were heard approaching he discovered Pamphilus standing beside him, as silent as himself.

Mysis herded the shuffling and stumbling company before her as best she could. Philocles walked with lifted knees, as children do in a procession. In one hand he held some grasses and with the other he clutched the mantle of his companion, the old door-keeper; but he was continually straying off, or standing still to gaze with wide dazzled eyes at the torches that preceded him or at the laughing by-standers. Behind him the deaf and dumb Ethiopian girl could scarcely be restrained from running forward to walk beside her sleeping friend, Chrysis, whose rebuke had been so terrible when she had done wrong and whose smile had been sufficient compensation for her imprisonment in silence. Glycerium walked with lowered eyes, lost to hope and lost to the decorum that now required of her the wailing and the distraught gestures of a conspicuous mourner. All these passed forward under the bright stars that had received the first intimation of day and shone with a last heightened brilliance, and under the long garlands of smoke that hung above the company in that windless air.

As the onlookers accompanied the procession into the open country, Simo's attention was fixed upon Glycerium, by reason of her condition, which was apparent to all, of her resemblance to her sister, of the dejection that invested her, and of the beauty and modesty of her bearing. And he became aware that his son also was watching the girl. In fact, during the whole journey, Pamphilus bent upon her his burning eyes, trying to intercept her glance and to communicate to her his encouragement and his love. But not until they reached the heaped-up wood whereon the bodies of a goat and a lamb were laid beside that of Chrysis, and not until the fire had touched it, did she raise her eyes. Then as the sound of the wailing increased in shrillness and the sound of the flute floated

piercingly above all, she turned to Mysis and began to speak wildly
into her ear. But the words of her vehemence were not heard in
that din, nor were Mysis's words of encouragement. Glycerium
was trying to draw herself away from the supporting arm of the
other and the slow faltering struggle of the two women was
lighted up by the rising flames. Pamphilus, in the intensity of his
concentration upon the suffering of the girl, moved slowly forward, his hands held out before him. And now he heard the words
that she was repeating: "It's best. It's best so!" Suddenly Glycerium pushed the older woman away from her and with a loud
cry of "Chrysis!" stumbled forward to fling herself upon the body
of her sister.

But Pamphilus had foreseen this attempt. Running across the
sand, he seized her by her disheveled hair and drew her back and
into his arms. The touch of that encircling arm released her tears.
She laid her head against his breast as one who had been there
before and was returning home.

The scandal of this embrace was felt at once by all the by-
standers and chiefly by Chremes, who turned upon Simo with his
protest and astonishment. But Simo had moved away and was
walking slowly home through the breaking dawn. Now he understood the Pamphilus of the last months.

The islanders discussed interminably the surprising event that
had taken place at Chrysis's funeral. They watched with hushed
excitement the chill that had fallen across the relations between the
families of Simo and of Chremes. Rumor presently asserted that
Pamphilus had promised to acknowledge the child, though no one,
naturally, even discussed the possibility of a marriage. Readers of a
later age will not be able to understand the difficulties that beset
the young man. Marriage was not then a sentimental relation, but
a legal one of great dignity, and the bridegroom's share in the

contract involved not so much himself as his family, his farm, and
his ancestors. Without the support of his parents and without a
residence in their home a young man was a mere adventurer,
without social, economic or civil standing. A marriage was only
possible if Simo declared it to be so. The customs of the islands
encouraged fathers in the luxuries of blustering and tyranny, but
Simo's relations with his son had always been strangely impersonal. He was confused by his own deference for his son, by what
he thought was his own weakness. Yet Simo's silence did not have
the air of a final refusal; it even seemed to imply that the decision,
with all its possibilities of lifetime regret and of a lifetime's
contention on the farm, rested with Pamphilus.

One day several months after Chrysis's funeral Pamphilus be-
took himself to the palaestra for some exercise. He entered the low
door and, nodding to a group of friends that sat scuffling under an
awning at the edge of the enclosure, he walked across the hot red
sand. The old attendant at the door who had won a laurel wreath
in his youth came trotting across the burning ring after him and as
soon as Pamphilus had seated himself on a marble bench began
kneading his calves and ankles. In the centre of the field Chremes's
son was going through the motions of hurling an imaginary
discus; thirty and fifty times he turned with lifted knee, trying to
fix in his muscular memory the perfect synchronization of the
gestures. Two other young men were practicing a festival dance,
interrupting their work from time to time to criticize one another's
slightest deviation from a harmonious balance. The young priest
of Aesculapius and Apollo was running around the course. Pamphilus sent the attendant away and lying down on his cloak let the
sunlight beat upon him. He did not think about his problem, but
left his mind a blank, suffused with a dull misery that identified
itself with the drowsy heat. Presently he placed his elbow on the

ground and raising his head rested his cheek upon his hand and
watched the priest of Apollo.

The priest never entered the competitive games, but he was
undoubtedly first upon the island for endurance and second only to
Pamphilus in swiftness. Save on the days of festival he appeared
for exercise daily and ran six miles. He preserved a perfect temperance: he drank no wine; he lived on fruit and vegetables; he
awoke with the sun and unless there was some call to attend the
sick he went to sleep with it. He had taken the vow of chastity, the
vow that forever closes the mind to the matter, without wistful
backglancing and without conceding the possibility that circumstance might yet present a harmless deviation, the vow which,
when profoundly compassed, fills the mind with such power that it
is forever cut off from the unstable tentative sons of men. His
office required his passing so much time among the sick and the
distressed that he had become inadequate to the cheerful and the
happy and no one on the island knew him very well. But he had a
strange power over the sick and the demented and only in their
hours of confession and despair was the shutter of his impersonality lifted; such as had known him then followed him ever after
with their eyes, in gratitude and in astonishment. He was only
twenty-eight, but he had been sent to Brynos by the priests that
attended the great mysteries of Athens and Corinth as a signal
honor; for the shrine on Brynos was one of particular significance
in the legend of Aesculapius and his father Apollo. Pamphilus
had never spoken to him beyond the salutations of the field, but he
would rather have known him than anyone in the world, and he in
turn watched Pamphilus with grave interest. Now Pamphilus lay
following him with his eyes and wishing he had his own life to
live over again.

Suddenly he became aware that someone was shaking him by the shoulder. It was one of his companions. "Here comes your father," said the boy and went back to the awning. Pamphilus rose to his feet and waited respectfully as Simo approached, preceded by the old attendant.

"Stay where you are. Lie down again," said Simo; "I'll sit here on this bench. I want to talk to you."

Pamphilus lay down, his face turned away towards the track.

Simo wiped his face with the hem of his skirt. "I won't be long, my boy. . . . But we must consider this matter somehow . . . after all." He was not sure of himself. He blew his nose. He coughed several times and roughly adjusted the folds of his gown. He repeated "Very well" and "Now" and waited in vain for Pamphilus to say something. At last he launched forth among his prepared introductions:

"Well now, my boy, I assume you want to marry the girl. Hm . . ."

Pamphilus put his head down between his folded arms as though he were going to sleep. He sighed in anticipation of all the irrelevancies he was about to hear. In his heart he knew he had only to say yes or no and his father would accede to his wish.

"I don't wish to coerce you. I think you are old enough to see the good and the bad for yourself. But for a few moments now I want to talk all around the matter. I want to put the other side of the case in its plainest terms and leave it there for a while. May I do that?"

"Yes," said Pamphilus.

"Well, to begin with, it's only right to face the fact that there is no outward obligation to marry the girl. I've looked into the matter. She is not a Greek citizen. She happens to have been brought up in a sheltered manner, or so I take it. This Chrysis seems to have tried to prevent the girl's falling into her way of life; but that does not alter the fact that she is a mere dancing girl. Now, mind you, I can see that she is modest and well-mannered. She appears to be just such a person as our own Argo. But she could never have hoped for anything above the situation she is now in. The world is full of just such likable stray girls as this Glycerium, but we cannot be expected to welcome them into the fabric of good Greek family life. You may be sure that Chrysis knew perfectly well that Glycerium must some day become a hetaira like herself, or a servant."

Simo paused. He could see the back only of his son's head, but he was able to imagine upon his face the set unhappy expression they had all been obliged to watch there for the last weeks. He coughed again and abruptly flung himself upon another of his openings:

"No doubt you feel yourself fairly bound to her by a promise— but a promise, Pamphilus, in which you failed to consider the rest of us, and especially your mother. If you decided to marry the girl, your mother and sister would try to live with her as peaceably as possible, we know; but it would be a good deal to ask of them. You know them. This girl does not understand the first thing about our island manners. She doesn't know how simple and monotonous our women's lives are. I expect that life with the Andrian and with that strange company at the house on the hill was an odd affair. She'd be unhappy with us. And even if she didn't contradict your mother all day . . . and worse . . . she'd become silent and sullen. Pamphilus, they would never grow fond of one another. It would be better to be cruel to her now and let her alone, than to set up discord, a lifetime of discord on our farm."

For a moment his memory failed him, but he rallied and continued:

"Well, even assuming that your mother and sister came to like her and to accept her cordially in the home, all her life she would have to endure something insulting in the manner of the other women on the island. We men do not take that interest in social discrimination, my son, but women . . . women with their few interests and . . . and so on . . . they enjoy having someone to ignore or to stare down. It warms them. Glycerium is not a Greek citizen. Her sister was a hetaira. All her life she would be obliged to endure their looking at her with straight lips and (I can see them) with half-closed eyes. But even that is not the chief thing."

He hoped that the suspense in this splendid transition would be reflected in some change in his son's position, but the young man lay motionless. Simo's weary eyes turned slowly about the palaestra.

"The girl is not strong. The women of the village seem to know something about it. She's a quick nervous high-strung girl and she'd bring you a series of thin and sickly children. You and I know those homes. She's not unlike our neighbor Douro's wife; isn't she? and the uneven health of such women—even though they're often more likable, yes, more likable, than the Philumenas —takes the shape of complaining and quarrelsomeness. And in their children. One has no right to bring into the world those children that cannot join others in their games, silent children who go through life regularly subject to fevers and coughs and pains. The most important thing in life is a houseful of strong healthy boys. Take Philumena, now. You do not 'love' Philumena, as the poets use the word. Well, when I married your mother perhaps I did not 'love' her in that sense. But I grew to love her and . . . euh . . . now I cannot imagine myself as having been married to anyone else, as satisfactorily married to anyone else. Philumena is handsome. But most important of all, Philumena is strong. So . . . so, Pamphilus, does what I am saying seem to have some truth in it? . . . Pamphilus?"

But Pamphilus had fallen asleep.

His last thought had been the recollection of one of Chrysis's maxims, an ironic phrase which he had chosen to take literally: *The mistakes we make through generosity are less terrible than the gains we acquire through caution.*

Simo was not vexed. He sighed. Looking up he saw the priest of Aesculapius and Apollo running around the course. He recalled the day several months before when he and Sostrata had taken Pamphilus's sister to the temple. For two days and two nights, Argo had been suffering from an ear-ache, and although they knew that the priest was often ungracious when his attention was asked on smaller ills they ventured to present her to him. The hour at which he was accustomed to receive the sick was a little after sunrise and there they found his colony. There were invalids brought to him on beds; there were sufferers from tumors, from protracted languors, from sore eyes; there were the possessed. Simo and Sostrata had passed their lives without ailments. They regarded them, like poverty, like uncleanliness, as mere bad citizenship; they were on the point of returning home, so great was their distaste for such manifestations. The priest required that the guardians who had brought their sick to him should retire to a distance during his interviews, and Simo and Sostrata had withdrawn with an ill grace to a nearby grove. Argo seemed not to share her parents' revulsion from these matters; even before she approached the place (her fingers pressed upon her ear) she had been subdued to awe and when her turn came she told her little story with caught breath. The priest gently touched her ear, recit-

ing a charm. He poured in some oil and looked deeply into her shy
eyes. And gradually as he gazed at her a smile appeared upon his
lips and slowly she smiled in return. True influence over another
comes not from a moment's eloquence nor from any happily
chosen word, but from the accumulation of a lifetime's thoughts
stored up in the eyes. And there is one thing greater than curing a
malady and that is accepting a malady and sharing its acceptance.
The ear-ache did not abate at once, but Argo pretended to her
parents that it did, for the other healing they would not have
understood; and all night long instead of complaining she pressed
against her ear the little bag of laurel leaves he had given her and
talked to herself, rehearsing that interview and that glance. Thereafter she never had any conversation with the priest, but when she
happened to meet him upon the road, her heart was filled with
excitement; she gave him a shy greeting and her eyelids fluttered in
a quick intimate glance and he in turn let fall upon her a faint
allusion to his smile. Her parents were amused by this bond; the
priest had brought out in their daughter a side they had never
known in her, and one that sent messages all along her life.
Henceforth she even stood up straighter. One day a cousin who
lived on the other side of the island came to a meal with them and
let fall a remark in disparagement of the priest, saying that he was
a comfort chiefly to old women who imagined themselves to be ill.
Argo's eyes grew dark and her lips straight with anger. She
refused to eat another mouthful and forever after the poor foolish
cousin could never draw a word from her and never knew why. All
this now returned to Simo's mind as he watched the priest.

"People like that," he thought to himself, "have some secret
about living. Why don't they tell it to us outright, instead of
wrapping it up in mystery and ceremonial? They know something
that prevents their blundering about, as we do. Yes, what am I

doing here," he added, pushing out his lower lip, "but playing the fool? Blundering, advising in things I know nothing about." He looked long at his sleeping son. "Pamphilus has some of that secret, too. And that woman from Andros had it, too. Chremes was right, though he meant it ill: there is something of the priest in Pamphilus, something of the priest trying to make its way in him. Let me get up and go away before I say anything more."

So he arose and a little guiltily left the field.

Pamphilus's mind was all but made up, yet still under the burden of perplexity and self-reproach he decided to seek still more light on his problem and a last reassurance by reviving a custom that had been in frequent use among the Greeks of the great age, but which had fallen off at the time of the events of this story. It consisted merely in abstaining from speech and from food from one sunrise to the next and in either passing the night in the temple enclosure or in arriving there before the dawn that closed the watch. There was not thought to be any particular magic in the practice: it cleared the mind of bodily fumes, it removed it from the commerce of the day and prepared it perhaps for a significant dream. The watcher guarded his fast and his silence, but the Greek mind did not approve of heightening the experience by any further self-denial. One moved about the home as usual, exercised in the palaestra or worked at the loom; one slept. If some uninformed person spoke to the watcher, he drew his finger across his lips and the condition of the vow was understood. Athletes still observed it several days before a race; brides on the eve of their wedding; old ladies who hoped to recover some lost trinket, or to recapture in a dream the features of some all-but-forgotten love; and devout soldiers about to set forth upon an expedition. It was indeed little short of odd that a healthy young man in the even current of life should revive this custom, but the islanders were still sufficiently

religious to respect the habits that had expressed the spiritual life
of their glorious grandfathers, and made no comment.

By mid-afternoon hunger had gained upon him and his dejection had increased a hundred-fold. Whichever choice he made
would involve the unhappiness of others. Under the weight of the
alternatives even the memory of Glycerium lost for a time any
tender association. He climbed over the remoter parts of the island,
gazing absently out to sea and idly plucking the grasses among the
rocks where he sat. He came to the spot where he had first seen
Glycerium and stood for a time, quiet as the stones about him,
asking himself whether the associations in life are based upon an
accidental encounter or upon a profound and inner necessity.
When he returned to the farm his mother and sister felt the
desolation that invested him and moved about with hushed steps.
The very slaves went about their tasks on tiptoe and finally withdrew in silence and in alarmed interrogation. During the evening
meal Pamphilus sat by the door with closed eyes. His brother,
returning, stepped over his feet with awed circumspection (he too
had made the watch only a few months before, but in pomp, with
twelve other youths on the occasion of their enrollment in the
League) and held himself at a distance, rendered uncomfortable by
so much seriousness in a good athlete. Of her own accord Argo
brought Pamphilus a bowl of water which he drank, smiling the
while intimately into her grave eyes; she returned to her place at
the table with great dignity and with secret excitement, as though
she had done something conspicuous. When Simo finally told
her and her brother to go to bed she slipped up to her father
and laid her lips against his ear: "What is it, father?" she
whispered. "No, tell me, what is the matter?" He took her hands
and played with them a moment; he raised his eyebrows wisely and
told her to go to bed and sleep well. From her bed in the darkness

she noted the movements of the family: that her mother took a
cloak and went out into the garden by the cliff, and that later her
father did the same. With wide eyes and cautious lifted ear she
followed this unaccustomed nocturnal roaming. She was filled with
loving excitement; she kissed her doll many times with violence
and wept. She became aware that her younger brother was venturing on hands and knees towards the moonlight in the court: she
too ventured out and they stared at one another, but Pamphilus
suddenly loomed up from the shadows and waved them back to
their beds.

Pamphilus wandered about the outer court. Again the moon was
at the full, throwing a milky blue mist over the tiers of olive trees
that climbed the hill across the road and casting black shadows
among the farm buildings. Its serenity contrasted strangely with
the mysterious excitement it awakened among the human beings it
fell upon. Pamphilus had seen his parents go into the garden, but
he saw them now without emotion, without pity. He returned to
the house and lay down upon his bed. Never had he been possessed by mood further from illumination. Lying on his face he
traced outlines upon the floor with his finger.

The shells gleamed on the path as Simo walked up and down;
from time to time he cast a furtive glance at his wife. She was
sitting on a bench of chipped and stained marble that had been his
mother's favorite seat. It had been placed there generations before,
under a fig arbor blown down long since on a night of legendary
storm. It stood at the very end of the garden where a cliff broke
down to the sea, and from it one could hear forever the long
spreading whispers of the ebbing and the rising waves below.
From that seat his mother had directed the bringing up of five
children, had dried their tears and listened with nodding head to
the absurd procession of their shifting enthusiasms. "Viewed from

a distance," Simo said to himself, "life is harmonious and beautiful. No doubt the years when my mother smiled to us from that bench were as full of crossed wills and exasperations as today, but how beautiful they seem in memory! The dead are wrapped in love; in illusion, perhaps. They go underground and slowly this tender light begins to fall upon them. But the present remains: this succession of small domestic vexations. I have lived such a life for sixty years and I am still upset by its ephemeral decisions. And I am still asking myself which is the real life: the present with its discontent, or the retrospect with its emotion?" He looked again guardedly at Sostrata, who sat fingering the folds of her cloak and expressing in every line of her position her unfriendliness and her rebellion. "The fault is in me," he continued. "If I were wiser, I could do this thing. As the head of the family I should be firmer. I should say 'yes' or 'no' clearly and let Pamphilus bring in his little girl. I should weed out all these hesitations. Even now she is waiting for me to make up her mind for her; if I spoke distinctly, even against her will, she would adjust herself without great effort. The house would find a way of accepting the new member and things would run on smoothly enough." He was thinking of going toward her with smiling affection, suggesting that at sixty they had earned the right to remain tranquil though the house fell; but he foresaw that her pride would not accommodate itself to any such resignation, and he continued up and down the garden.

Indeed Sostrata did not wish Simo to speak to her. Her mind was filled with one long obstinate exclamation at the stupidity of men. Only a woman's mind could foresee all the harm that would result from such a marriage as the one now being weighed. It was the women of the island that had measured all danger that came with the arrival of the Alexandrian woman; and now she, the first matron of Brynos, was being ordered to receive into her home the last offscouring of that dispersed colony. She had anticipated all her life the rich satisfactions of being a mother-in-law and a grandmother, though what she anticipated was a daughter-in-law of straw. A Greek HOME, she knew, was the only breakwater against the tide of oriental manners, of financial fluctuation, and of political chaos. The highest point toward which any existence could aspire was to be a member of an island family, living and dying on one farm, respected, cautious, and secretly wealthy; of a family stretching into the past as far as the mossy funerary urns could record, and into the future as far as the imagination could reach, that is to one's grandchildren. Society was similarity. These things she repeated to herself, and under the waves of her indignation and self-pity—though the greater part of the time she stood in awe of her husband and her son—all her gracious traits disappeared, her beautiful eyes became harsh that for three days had been bright with the angry tears of her inner monologue.

When after a long stretch of time Simo paused in his walk and approached her with deferential hesitation, she arose abruptly and walked past him into the house, breathing hard and trembling with excitement.

At last Pamphilus arose and throwing his fleece-lined cloak over his shoulder slowly and musingly walked through the little garden in the court and passed through the outer gates of the farm. He was strangely light-headed from hunger and dejection. He paused for a moment to gaze at the rising hillside before him and its silvered olive trees. To his eyes they seemed to be pulsating in even waves of intensity, as though the whole earth and sky were on fire and burning with a pale slow silver flame, the whole earth and sky, unconsumed yet incessantly feeding the countless tongues of flame. He was gazing at this serene conflagration when he became aware of two dim figures in a pool of profound shadow at his right, leaning against the pillar of the gate. Glycerium was pressing her cheek against the stone and breathing her prayer toward the house within and beside her Mysis, distraught and helpless, stood urging her mistress to return home and to leave the ominous vapors of the night and the jealous chill of the moon.

When Glycerium saw that Pamphilus was standing in the road and that he had recognized her, she drew back into Mysis's arms overcome with shame; but slowly collecting herself she stretched forward a hand to him and fixed her great eyes imploringly on his face.

Mysis whispered to her: "We must go home, my bird, my treasure."

"Pamphilus," said Glycerium, "help me!"

His heart contracted within him as he realized the extremity of suffering that had led her thus far. He laid his finger gravely across his lips. He did not smile, but approaching her he looked down into her face with earnest reassurance and beckoned her to accompany Mysis toward the town.

Glycerium pushed back the scarf from her forehead and fell upon one knee before him, babbling incoherently: "I love you. I love you, Pamphilus. You promised me that you loved me. What am I to do? What is to become of me?"

Pamphilus looked at Mysis and again drew his finger across his mouth.

"Hush, my darling," she said. "You see he has taken the vow and cannot speak to us. And we must not speak to him. Look, he wants you to start home with me." She put her arm about the girl's waist and they began to move slowly toward the road.

"He promised me that he loved me," muttered Glycerium,

unable to see for her tears, but permitting herself to be led forward. After a few steps, however, she turned and, pushing Mysis aside, said: "No, no! I wish to see him again." She pressed her scarf against her mouth for a moment and gazed at him, her whole soul in her eyes: "Pamphilus, do not marry me, if it is not right. But do not leave me alone. Do not leave me so long alone. Remember Chrysis. Remember the day you found me being stoned by the boys. No, no, do not marry me, if your father and your mother do not wish it, but let me know that . . . that I am still loved by you."

At last he nodded and smiled and waved to her slowly.

"He is nodding his head, Mysis!" cried Glycerium.

"Yes, my treasure."

"Look, Mysis, he is smiling at me. Can you see? Look very hard, Mysis."

"See, now he is waving to you. Wave to him again."

Glycerium waved eagerly, like a child, until Pamphilus was out of sight. It was a long walk home over uneven stones. Glycerium talked excitedly of the smile, trying to estimate the exact shade of intention and affection that lay in his waving to her and in the nod of his head. They discussed the significance of his taking the vow and they talked in general of the custom of taking the vow and recalled all the occasions they could remember of this usage and the results of each occasion. "All will be well, Mysis," she repeated feverishly. "You will see, believe me, all will be well." But finally they fell silent, and in the silence their fears returned and an overwhelming weariness. As they reached the door of their house, Glycerium paused with tight-drawn lower lip and with fear in her eyes: "There is nothing to hope for," she said. "The gods are angry because I thought for a time that I was happy and that the world was easy to live in. At that time I did not understand

anything about life and I said cruel things to Chrysis, because I
thought the world was easy to live in. And the gods are right. Oh,
if I could speak to her for only one moment and could tell her that
now I understand her goodness, her goodness. But Chrysis is
dead!" She turned to Mysis, but at these words Mysis had withdrawn from her and, beating upon her forehead with the knuckles
of her two hands, had fallen upon the threshold of the house.

Pamphilus continued in the opposite direction. He wandered
about the upland pastures as he had done all day, and climbed to
the highest point on the island to gaze upon the moon and the sea.
He tried to lift his mind out of the narrow situation of his
problem by thinking of things not before him. He thought of the
ships that under that magical flowing light were making their way
from port to port, each one casting aside at its prow two glistening
murmurous waves. It was the hour when the helmsman in the
security of the course falls into a revery, remembers his childhood
or reckons up his savings. Pamphilus thought of the thousands of
homes over all Greece where sleeping or waking souls were forever
turning over the dim assignment of life. "Lift every roof," as
Chrysis used to say, "and you will find seven puzzled hearts." He
thought of Chrysis and her urn, and remembered her strange
command to him that he praise all life, even the dark. And as he
thought of her his depression, like a cloud, drifted away from him
and he was filled with a tremulous happiness. He too praised the
whole texture of life, for he saw how strangely life's richest gift
flowered from frustration and cruelty and separation. Chrysis
living and Chrysis dying in pain; the thoughtful glance that his
father so often let rest upon him and the weary expression on his
father's face when he thought himself unobserved; the shy mystery
of Glycerium. It seemed to him that the whole world did not

consist of rocks and trees and water nor were human beings
garments and flesh, but all burned, like the hillside of olive trees,
with the perpetual flames of love,—a sad love that was half hope,
often rebuked and waiting to be reassured of its truth. But why
then a love so defeated, as though it were waiting for a voice to
come from the skies, declaring that therein lay the secret of the
world. The moonlight is intermittent and veiled, and it was under
such a light that they lived; but his heart suddenly declared to him
that a sun would rise and before that sun the timidity and the
hesitation would disappear. And as he strode forward this truth
became clearer and clearer to him and he laughed because he had
been so long blind to what was so obvious. He strode forward, his
arms raised to the sky in joyous gratitude, and as he went he cried:
"I praise all living, the bright and the dark."

The exhilaration gave place finally to a tranquil fatigue. As he
entered the shadowy temple he saw the priest sleeping before the
altar he tended. The priest opened his eyes a moment and above
the curve of his arm he watched the young man spread his cloak
upon the marble pavement and lie down upon it and fall asleep.

Simo was awakened a little before dawn by the sounds of shrill
voices and of unaccustomed movement in the outer courtyard. On
approaching he discovered that a clamorous old woman had
entered the gates and that a number of his slaves were trying in
vain to quiet her and to drive her back into the road. He recognized Mysis. With a gesture he commanded the men to release her.
"What is the matter?" he asked.

"I must see Pamphilus."

"He is not here."

"I cannot go away until I have seen him," she replied, her voice

rising in feverish insistence. "A life depends upon it. I do not care
what happens to me, but Pamphilus must know what they have
done to us."

Simo said quietly: "I shall have you whipped; I shall have you
shut up in a room for three days, if you continue to make this
noise. Pamphilus will be able to listen to you later in the morning."

Mysis was silent a moment, then she raised her eyes and said
sombrely: "Later in the morning will be too late, and all will be
lost. I beg of you to let me see him now. He would wish it. He
would not forgive you for turning me away now."

"Come, tell me what is the matter and I will help you."

"No, it is you who have done this harm and now he alone can
save us."

Simo sent the slaves back to their quarters. Then he turned to
her again: "In what way have I harmed you?"

"You do not wish to help us," she said. "The Leno's boat has
arrived at the island and my mistress Glycerium and all the household of Chrysis have been sold to him as slaves. We were
awakened in the middle of the night by the herald of the village
and told to gather our clothes together and to go down to the
harbor. Glycerium is not well now; she must not be driven so. I
myself escaped through the rows of a vineyard and have come to
find Pamphilus. It was you who have done this, for it was the
Fathers of the Island who ordered that we should be sold as slaves
to pay our debts."

This was true. He remembered having listened without interest
to a discussion of the matter, assuming that it would be carried out
with sufficient warning and delay to admit of Glycerium's being
separated from the rest of the destitute company. The Leno's boat
visited Brynos so seldom that it seemed to the Fathers of the Island

that it they might yet be under the necessity of providing for the household through many months while awaiting the arrival of this purchaser.

Suddenly a light dawned upon Mysis: "He is at the temple! How could I have forgotten that he was under the vow of silence and that he must be there!" And turning she started to enter the road.

"You must not go to him at the temple," said Simo sharply. "I shall come down to the harbor with you now and buy your mistress from the Leno."

He returned to the house for his cloak, then walked into the town with Mysis hurrying at his heels. Dawn was breaking as he descended the winding stairs to the square. Against the streaked sky he saw the mast of the Leno's boat. The Leno was not only a dealer in slaves; he was a wandering bazaar and sold foreign foods and trinkets and cloths. If an island were large enough he came ashore and conducted a fair and a circus. And now in the first cold light of morning Simo could see on the raised portion of the deck a brightly colored booth, a chained bear, an ape, two parrots, and other samples of the Leno's stock in trade, including the household of Chrysis. Philocles had remained on shore and for two hours had been standing at the parapet uttering short broken cries towards his companions. Being a Greek citizen he could not be sold into slavery and was to be transported later to Andros.

Simo descended the steps of the landing with Mysis and was rowed out to the boat. While he concluded his transaction with the black and smiling Leno Mysis sank upon her knees before Glycerium, telling her of this good fortune. But Glycerium derived no joy from the news. She sat between Apraxine and the Ethiopian girl, amid the bundles of their clothes, and for weariness she could scarcely raise her eyes or move her lips. "No," she said, "I shall stay here with you. I do not wish to go anywhere."

Simo approached them. "My child," he said to Glycerium, "you are to come with me now."

"Yes, my beloved," Mysis repeated into her ear, "you must go with him. All will be well. He is taking you ashore to Pamphilus."

Still Glycerium remained with bent head. "I do not wish to move. I do not wish to go anywhere," she said.

"I am the father of Pamphilus. You must come with me and good care will be taken of you."

At last and with great difficulty she arose. Mysis supported her to the side of the boat and there taking her farewell she whispered to her: "Goodbye, my dear love. Now may the gods bring you happiness. I shall never see you again, but I pray you to remember me, for I have loved you well. And wherever we are, let us remember our dear Chrysis."

The two women embraced one another in silence, Glycerium with closed eyes. At last she said: "I would that I were dead, Mysis. I would that I were long dead with Chrysis, my dear sister."

"You are to come with us too," said Simo to Mysis, who having known even greater surprises obediently followed him. The little group was rowed in silence to the shore. The Leno's oarsmen struck the water, his bright colored sails were raised, and his merchandise left the harbor for other fortunes.

The sun had already risen when Pamphilus returned with swift and happy steps to his home. There he discovered Glycerium sleeping peacefully under his mother's care. There was not a sound to be heard on the farm, for his mother, already invested with the dignity of her new duties as guardian and nurse to the outcast girl, had ordered a perfect quiet. Argo was sitting before the gate, her eyes wide with wonder and pleasure at the arrival of this new friend. Simo had gone to the warehouse and when he returned, for all his happiness, he moved about with lowered eyes, driven by the constraint in his nature to act as though nothing had happened.

In the two days that followed, all their thoughts were centred about the room where the girl lay and all their hearts were renewed under the fragile claims that Glycerium's beauty and shyness made upon them. Simo seemed, after Pamphilus, to have best understood her reticence and to have been understood by her; a friendship beyond speech had grown up between them. This flowering of goodness, however, was not to be put to the trial of routine perseverance, nor to know the alternations of self-reproach and renewed courage; for on the noon of the third day Glycerium's pains began and by sunset both mother and child were dead.

That night after many months of drought it began to rain. Slowly at first and steadily, the rain began to fall over all Greece. Great curtains of rain hung above the plains; in the mountains it fell as snow, and on the sea it printed its countless ephemeral coins upon the water. The greater part of the inhabitants were asleep, but the relief of the long-expected rain entered into the mood of their sleeping minds. It fell upon the urns standing side by side in the shadow, and the wakeful and the sick and the dying heard the first great drops fall upon the roofs above their heads. Pamphilus lay awake, face downward, his chin upon the back of his hand. He heard the first great drops fall upon the roof over his head and he knew that his father and mother, not far from him, heard them too. He had been repeating to himself Chrysis's lesson and adding to it his Glycerium's last faltering words: "Do not be sorry; do not be afraid," and he had been remembering how with the faintest movement of her eyes to one side, she had indicated her child and said: "Wherever we are, we are yours." He had been asking himself in astonishment wherein had lain his joy and his triumph of the few nights before: how could he have once been so sure of the beauty of existence? And some words of Chrysis returned to him. He recalled how she had touched the hand of a young guest who had returned from an absence, having lost his sister, and how she had said to him in a low voice, so as not to embarrass those others present who had never known a loss: "You were happy with her once; do not doubt that the conviction at the heart of your happiness was as real as the conviction at the heart of your sorrow." Pamphilus knew that out of these fragments he must assemble during the succeeding nights sufficient strength, not only for himself, but for these others,—these others who so bewilderingly now turned to him and whose glances tried to read from his face what news there was from the last resources of courage and hope, to live on, to live by. But in confusion and with flagging courage he repeated: "I praise all living, the bright and the dark."

On the sea the helmsman suffered the downpour, and on the high pastures the shepherd turned and drew his cloak closer about him. In the hills the long-dried stream-beds began to fill again and the noise of water falling from level to level, warring with the stones in the way, filled the gorges. But behind the thick beds of clouds the moon soared radiantly bright, shining upon Italy and its smoking mountains. And in the East the stars shone tranquilly down upon the land that was soon to be called Holy and that even then was preparing its precious burden.

Format by Katharine Sitterly
Set in Intertype Garamond
Composed, printed and bound by American Book–Stratford Press, Inc.
HARPER & ROW, PUBLISHERS, INCORPORATED